Gifted

an anthology

Edited by Debz Hobbs-Wyatt and Gill James

Bridge House

British Library Cataloguing in Publication Data

A Record of this Publication is available from the British
Library

ISBN 978-1-914199-50-9

This edition published 2023 by Bridge House Publishing
Manchester, England

Contents

Introduction

It has become somewhat of a tradition here at Bridge House, to set the theme of our yearly anthology loosely connected to Christmas – while at the same time such that it is open to interpretation. This means the stories can be set any time. *Gifted* is no exception and when we set it as our theme, hoped for a rich array of stories that explored the many interpretations of a gift. We were not disappointed. Choosing which ones worked best as a collection was the hardest part and like every year, we had to reject some great stories. Not because we didn't love the writing, but sometimes it simply comes down to how well the theme is interpreted and often it's more about how it fits in a collection. We don't want too many stories with the same or similar use of the theme. This is always tricky and the choice is often subjective, although we do now have a scoring system to try to make this as objective as it can be. Not easy in a creative field.

Once again, it's interesting how many familiar names show up when we've made our selection and had the joy of uncovering the name of the author (something we only look at after we've chosen) and always a pleasure to see some new names. So, we are delighted once again to welcome back some writers you will already know as well as some new writers, some making their publishing debut – often after many years of honing the craft. The short story form is an often-over-looked art form and one that requires a lot of dedication and hard work. It might be shorter than the novel but there is a brevity of language and sharpness of style that is not easy to fit into so few words. Short stories are complete stories with characters we come to care about and with meanings explored and left to linger beyond the pages. That is not so easy to do when you have so few words to play with – so well done to all who made it here. And if you didn't – never give up, maybe next year.

You will read about gifts that we understand in the more traditional sense, though some too big to gift-wrap. You will read about gifts that are not so tangible – things that cannot be held in the hand. Every story has interpreted the theme in its own wonderful and interesting way and we hope you love the richly textured and well-written feast of stories that made it into our collection.

So, we implore you to sit back and enjoy the talents of our many gifted writers.

A Majestic Man

Alyson Faye

1985 Halifax, Yorkshire

The cinema was nearly empty, but then it was midnight and all the punters had gone home. The shutters had been pulled down. Mabel, after applying her usual extra coat of lipstick to her rouge red pout, as armour against the bus ride back, had departed, with the spare confectionery for her nephews and nieces. Only The Majestic's owner, Rigby Rogers, was left sitting in the front row, with a pair of swollen-bellied tubs of popcorn on either side, staring at the flickering monochrome images on the screen.

He liked to run his favourite films after hours; he'd always been a night owl. He was mouthing the dialogue along with the film's bleached-out figures, as he watched a fat be-hatted, bow-tied man alongside his sad-faced, scarecrow companion, tramp across a studio desert in boots and kepis. Their neck drapes were blowing back into their faces courtesy of the wind machines' breeze, all captured on nitrate nearly a hundred years before and thousands of miles away, across an ocean, in Hollywood. Their familiar antics flowed from the screen, flooding Rigby with nostalgia…

Halifax, 1960

A sick day and an escape from the hell of Rigby's daily life at the local secondary school. He was lying in bed, cosy, whilst hugging a hot water bottle wrapped in blue rubber, watching, as a rare daytime treat, the black and white portable TV.

"Let's watch Laurel and Hardy, son," his mum said.

The sound of her knitting needles interwoven with Hardy's high-pitched giggles and Laurel's sobs were a wonderful tonic.

His mum carried on. "I saw them, Mr Laurel and Mr Hardy, in person. Oh, about seven years ago in t' middle of town, at the old Odeon." The needles clicked. Rigby stared in amazement. "That Hardy fella, he was double the size, sweating buckets, the poor man. The thin fella, well, he looked like he'd not eaten in months. End of the road for them really."

Rigby fiddled with the patterned Paisley bedcover, hardly daring to believe that right here in his bedroom was a living link to these celluloid ghosts and his comedy heroes.

"Hung around the back door of the Odeon I did, for hours, but they didn't come out. Perhaps they were hiding?" Mum added, looking thoughtful.

"Who from?" Ten-year-old Rigby was confused.

"Dunno, Rigby. From Halifax? Or themselves? They couldn't have wanted to be here – not really? I mean – Hollywood to Halifax– it's the wrong way round that journey."

Dear old Mum, thought Rigby. She'd been dead these past ten years, but he still remembered her knitting needles, the luridly bright sweaters that grew from them and her stories.

Rigby roared with laughter, his face lit by the screen's silvery glow. He turned to the pair of figures standing at the head of each aisle.

"See, fellas, you've not lost the old magic. You're still making us laugh in Halifax."

The two silent companions – wooden, life-sized figures, one thin and sad-faced, Mr Stan Laurel, and the other rotund and bow-tied, Mr Oliver Hardy, stood upright, rigid and unbending, with painted lips and eyes.

They were quite the talking point for the cinema's customers, and Rigby, a familiar florid-faced figure, poised in the foyer, liked to tell everyone, "They were a gift, you know, from Mr Laurel. To The Majestic, when I opened in '62. He was born just over the border in Lancashire. He'd family there and used to visit. Especially after Mr Hardy died. One of them told him about me opening The Majestic and showing one of their films, so he sent these two fellas over. Worth a bomb now, I expect."

Rigby had told this fable so often he half-believed it and indeed, there were nuggets of truth woven into its warp and weft. Rigby was, as he saw it, in the business of selling dreams. He offered an escape for a couple of hours, from life's dreary toil, all the while sitting in red plush velvet seats holding hands in the dark with your beloveds.

"Gift of the gab, Mr R, is what you've got," his box office manageress, Mabel, often told him, fond but disapproving.

"What's the harm, luv? It's just another story. We've got a million of them here, trapped in the walls of this palace."

The L&H companions, with Rigby standing proud between them, had had their photograph in the local press, *The Courier*. Then, to everyone's surprise, a national picked up the story and ran with it. The phone started ringing at all hours, and the fans started turning up, knocking at the closed doors, hanging around the back alley, pestering for a chance to pose with the companions. Mr Laurel's gift. A piece of cinema history.

"It's getting out of hand now, Mr R.," Mabel said, one bleak Monday afternoon, as she patted her perm into place prior to pulling up the shutters on the box office. "They're camping outside overnight now. Look! And we're running out of Rowntrees fruit gums, they're eating them by the bucketload." She pointed at the scattering of tents and

11

umbrellas outside the glass doors cluttering up the pavement and the handkerchief-sized patch of grass.

"But it's good for business, Mabel. You can't deny the coffers have been filling up nicely. Usually it's very quiet at this time of year. Can't look a gift horse in the mouth, can we?"

Mabel lowered her voice, so the two lasses, training as usherettes, couldn't overhear. "But what if they find out it's all a... *fib*." She blushed. "You're charging them money to pose with Mr L and Mr H."

"And, just to remind you, Mabel, I'm giving you a cut."

Mabel blushed even deeper. With her Wilfred not working he was sure the extra shillings were coming in handy. No doubt they could have fish and chips and steak pie every week now, plus there were the perms, colour tints and little luxury treats from Harveys department store.

"Go on, girls," Rigby told the usherettes, "open up the doors, and let them in."

At midnight Rigby sat smoking in his office counting the evening's takings. A nearly empty bottle of whiskey sat beside him. He was a happy man, though, if he had to be honest, a tinge of guilt was taking the edge off his mellow mood. He hated having a conscience.

He stood up, flicked off the lights, and took his usual late-night promenade around the premises – up to the reels room where the camera lurked, and back down to the cloakrooms, box office, foyer, and then into the heart of The Majestic, the screening room.

The companions stood in their usual spots, silent, waiting.

"Nice work, lads. You've done me proud. What a gift you've turned out to be." He patted their wooden shoulders fondly.

Behind him the screen flowered into life, black and white images formed, familiar faces, staring out at him. Rigby turned around to face – Mr Laurel and Mr Hardy, but both were sad, and frowning, shaking their heads, saying, "No more, enough is enough. Respect our legacy, Rigby Rogers."

Rigby staggered backwards, and collapsed into one of the front-row seats, his heart pounding. In the dim light he believed he saw the companion figures moving towards him, heard the creak of wood, swore their arms lifted up to shake admonitory fingers... as they juddered nearer and nearer...

He woke up a few hours later, on the floor of the cinema, face down, blurry with the booze and a banging headache.

The screen was thankfully empty and dark, and the companions were in their usual spots, motionless.

Mabel arrived breathless, her hair still in rollers. She'd come straight over from "Curl and Cut". "What's the trouble, Mr R.? Why did you phone me at the hairdressers? Is there an emergency?"

Rigby sat behind his desk, feet up, sober, and shaved. "Film festival. That's the ticket. We're going to start a regular Laurel and Hardy film festival. Right here in Halifax, with photographs of when the boys toured here. Advertise for people's memories of them. Like me dear old late mum's. Get them interviewed and put up a little exhibition. Pull those fans in, give them a meal, too. Pie and peas. Open up the rooms upstairs and run their comedies over forty-eight hours. A weekender. I've realised that the greatest gift, Mabel, of Mr L and Mr H – their legacy – of laughter."

Mabel nodded, and out of the corner of her eye she could have sworn the two companions nodded too. Just a

13

tiny movement, and then – nothing. But their faces seemed brighter, as though the paint had been refreshed overnight.

About the author
Aly lives in the UK, with her family and rescue-Labrador, Roxy. She is a tutor, editor, mum, dog-walker, wild water swimmer and avid film buff.

Her fiction has been published widely – in *Space and Time* #141, Brigids Gate Press' *Were-Tales, Musings* and *Daughter of Sarpedon,* by Perpetual Motion in *Night Frights 2*, on *The Casket of Fictional Delights, Coffin Bell,* various *Sirens Call* e-zines, *World of Myth* and Unsettling Press' *Still of Night.*

Her stories can be downloaded on various podcasts, including this summer at *The Other Stories* as part of their Gothic showcase: *After the Gloaming* – https://pod.link/1693204342

Other film-related articles penned by her can be read here: https://alyrhodes-99284.medium.com

Her work has been read out on BBC Radio, local radio and won or placed in several competitions.

She is a regular on the West Yorkshire open mic circuit.

A Talented Artist

Jane Spirit

Suzie had not seen the postcard straight away. It must have got caught up in the pile of letters she had gathered up from the porch floor that morning. Bereavement seemed to have brought with it a tidal wave of correspondence from the outside world to match her own inner deluge of emotions. On that morning, just thinking about the demands the envelopes would contain had almost overwhelmed her. She had dropped the whole pile onto the breakfast bar whilst she went through the motions of making tea and drifting, cup in hand, across the tiled floor towards the kitchen's bifold doors. They framed her view of the extensive lawn with its carefully placed shrubs. Suzie found the organisation of the garden and the rest of the large ranch-style detached house reassuring. The place exuded an aura of order, of getting things done as well as of material success. It made her feel that somehow Martin was still busying about somewhere close by and hadn't died so suddenly three weeks ago.

She sipped her tea, distracted by the shards of memories that seemed to be all that was left of her fractured consciousness. In her mind's eye she was back in Edinburgh and stepping over the threshold of the little gallery where she had been invited to show a few of her art school paintings as part of their newcomers' exhibition. She remembered that she had been nervous at the exhibition opening. Her tutors had told her how gifted she was, but she remained uncertain about the worth of her ethereal, pastel-coloured canvases that were neither quite landscapes nor entirely abstract paintings. It was at that opening that she had first met Martin. Older than her and already a successful businessman, he had been introduced to her as an art lover.

"I love art, but I haven't a creative bone in my body," he had said, asking her to show him round her pictures.

Once she had taken him over to view them, he had sought her help. "Now I've seen your work, I can see that you understand how to reach into the mind of your viewer. I'd love to know more about how you do that, please?"

He had wooed her in that way, by making it all about her helping him, when in reality of course it was the other way round. It was Martin who had the good looks, bonhomie, and the confidence for the two of them. She had fallen in love with him and then married him because he was conventional about such matters and, if she were to be totally honest, because he could provide for her. She would be able to spend her time painting. She pictured her future self in her very own light-filled studio. Once there, she would finally know how to depict the undulating animal forms that had so far eluded her when she painted, but which existed ethereally somewhere within the pastel places of her imagination.

That was how she had come to be in the inner recesses of the museum sketching dead animals on a gloomy winter's afternoon. It was not very long after Martin had proposed to her on bended knee in their favourite champagne bar close to the gallery where they had met. Now, as she stood amongst random examples of Victorian taxidermy, she found herself fascinated by the way that they had been posed, as if caught during the gathering of nuts, or cleaning of whiskers. She was also awash with horror. Their zombie-like state of preservation was only possible because all the joyous imperfections of life had been sucked out of them.

Instinctively she had stepped backwards, bumping into a young man who was also carrying a sketch book. He simply smiled at her before asking her if she was alright, though it was she who had stepped on him.

16

"I'm Ian," he had said and then, "Are you going to sketch the big beast too?" gesturing towards the massive stag installed at the dim far end of the gallery.

The huge animal had been stuffed as if rising high on his hind legs, poised for battling, his antlers curved like some extraordinary modern candelabra. She had followed Ian down the gallery and watched him begin to draw the creature. Much to her surprise, Suzie had found herself sketching the outline of Ian's face, its youthfulness, rather messy hair, sharp nose, and intense eyes. He seemed unaware that she was drawing him as they talked about themselves. He was not an artist, but a zoology student.

"I suppose you could say that I'm drawn to places like this." He had laughed at his own pun.

Later they shared confidences with ease over cups of tea in the museum café. Suzie had told Ian that she would try to draw the stag in her own style because for her all art had more of life in it than any dead specimen, however well preserved. In return Ian had told her about his dream of one day tracking the living relatives of the gallery stag by tagging and studying the Barbary deer still to be found in Northern Africa. They had struck up a kind of friendship and she had even invited him to the wedding, though he hadn't come. It had been of no consequence to her really and she had soon abandoned her dream of painting any kind of stag-like creature. She had Martin after all. He too was always protecting his territory, flexing his muscles, asserting his prowess over younger contenders. Even his death had been decisive. He had been out enjoying some team-building shooting party when he had keeled over on the forest floor and could not be revived. As he had lain dying, she had been in her bright studio, painting. Although she no longer believed in the value of her fey little washes of faint colours, Martin had still admired them. He was always telling her how talented she was.

17

Martin, she thought, and turned back from the window suddenly as if he were somehow standing close behind her. Finding herself still alone, she placed her unfinished tea on the breakfast bar and listlessly began to sift through the post she had dumped there. She recognised the painting reproduced on the postcard immediately as Landseer's "The Monarch of the Glen" in which the stag looked down on the viewer defiantly through intensely dark eyes beneath sculpted antlers. She had read only recently that the picture had finally found its home in Edinburgh's National Gallery. The card could only have come from Ian. He must have heard about Martin and sent it as a curious kind of condolence letter.

She turned the card over and read the message written in Ian's cramped handwriting. "Big antlers don't always indicate a big heart." There were no other words and no signature. She felt an immediate flush of anger. What was he saying to her? Was he reminding her that Martin, for all his status in the world, had not really been capable of understanding her, of loving her? And what, Ian was? How dare Ian send it to her now to upset her so soon after Martin had died.

It was then that she noticed the stamp, a foreign one, and the date and place franked across it from Algeria. The card had been posted more than four weeks ago, well before Martin had died. It occurred to her that Ian had merely wanted to let her know that in his own quiet and unassuming way, he had not given up on his dream of travelling to track the wild deer of North Africa.

Unsure what to do next, Suzie propped the postcard up against her cup of cold tea and reached across the breakfast bar for a sketch pad and pencil she had left there months ago. She perched on a high stool and began to draw, feverishly copying the sinews of Landseer's image, absorbed now in her own vision of a deer, her own hart. She felt suddenly that

18

she had so much time to make up for and no time to waste in regretting what she had not done. She could think only of the lines and shadows in the world that she had not yet explored as now she would.

About the author:
Jane Spirit lives in Suffolk UK and has been inspired to start writing fiction by going along to her local creative writing class.

A Tenmoku Vase

Paul Harper-Scott

Soft pink clay flowed through the old woman's fingers. Two crooked claws, a knuckle bent outwards by arthritis, tissue-thin and leather-smooth skin. Leaning elbow to knee and watching by the side of the potter's wheel was a nineteen-year-old woman, her hair tied up in a ponytail. She raised her foot from the pedal to arrest the spinning of the wheel and reached forward to inspect the pot with her hands.

"This is much better, Pearl. Your walls are a very even thickness but you could still get some more of the weight out of the bottom of the clay." She restarted the wheel and reached into a bowl to gather water in her cupped hand, which she used to moisten the pot by pouring onto its rim. The water flowed in spiralling rivulets inside and out.

"Oh Wynn, my love, I've added another inch!" Pearl's face blossomed into the tracery of wrinkles that eighty-two years of laughter had crocheted into it: the merest twitch of her mouth could pull her features into a map of joy. As Pearl readied to lift the pot from the wheel and place it on a shelf, her shaking hand made her catch the base with her fingernail.

"Oh no, I've spoilt it." Her shoulders dropped, arching her back.

"Think of it as a decoration," said Wynn. "It's not a scratch: you've just created a blade of grass. Why don't you add a few more with the tip of this wooden knife? It'll look lovely if we use a dark tenmoku glaze. The glaze will break over the texture and show up orange against the black-brown of the rest of the vase."

Pearl raised an eyebrow.

"I'm not just saying it," Wynn continued. "Making accidents beautiful is what pottery is all about. The Japanese do something called *kintsugi*, which means using coloured glue to put broken pottery back together. They think its injuries tell the pot's unique story and make it lovelier. There's a craft shop in town where they do it professionally."

"Can you get me their number? My anniversary plate was broken soon after Jack died and I haven't had the heart to throw it away. I'd love to have it repaired."

Wynn's uncle worked at the old pottery in a fishing village on the north Cornish coast, and had taught her to throw pots when she was a bright but aimless girl of ten. Sitting alone in the workshop above the museum after the ceramics classes had finished, Wynn spent evenings throwing identical forms at the wheel, her muscle memory and ability to visualise the negative space around the pot increasing with each revolution of the wheel.

Wynn's father, a taxi driver whose income fluctuated hazardously with the seasonal variation in tourist numbers, had hoped that she might become an accountant, to make use of her ability with numbers. But Wynn excelled in most subjects, and her teachers pleaded with her to favour their subjects as she narrowed her study choices in preparation for university. English would be her degree discipline, if she achieved her grades, because (her uncle said) "You'll want something to fall back on in case there aren't any pottery jobs left. People don't value the old ways so much anymore."

The village's nursing home, part of a religious "hospital" run by a community of nuns, had a team of volunteers – Wynn was the youngest – to provide creative classes for its

21

residents. The ceramics class borrowed a wheel from the pottery workshop. There were two students: Pearl, and Agnes – who suffered from paralysis following a stroke and attended simply to watch.

"Some of the people who eat at the pub are really awful," Wynn said, as she pulled handles for Pearl out of a lump of clay that she was holding over a bowl of water. "They laugh at the conversations our regulars are having, and go on about how lucky we are to be able to live in palaces on the sea front for the same money they have to spend on their flats in London."

"It's youngsters like you these blooming emmets harm the most," cut in Agnes. "There's nobody your age can afford to buy anywhere here these days, it's so full of holiday homes."

"I know. Oh, there was one bloke last night that you'd probably have slapped if you'd been a few years younger. I overheard him berating me when I was waiting for the next-door table to make up its mind what it wanted to order, and he said, 'Jesus, she must be one of the most incapable waitresses I've ever encountered. Did you see the way she just gawped when you placed the order? And her knocking over the dogs' water bowl was the *pièce de resistance*. Nice arse, though.' "

"Oh Wynn, my lover, what a rat. I hope you got him with the water."

"Right, Pearl, let's pick a nice couple of these handles and get them onto your cups. We might even be able to persuade her to give one of them to you when they're done, Agnes."

In her first term at university, Wynn was scheduled for supervisions on critical writing with Dr Montagu. Slim, smart, and probably somewhere in his mid-forties, Montagu spoke with a studied prissiness that she had never encountered before coming to Cambridge. Supervisions were held in his college rooms, which were furnished with armchairs, a sofa, a coffee table obscured by ill-stacked piles of academic journals, and two full walls of bookcases. On the free walls were architectural drawings of the college buildings and a photo of Montagu as a student at a college ball.

"How do you read the opening stanza?" He had handed them a poem by John Donne at their first meeting. "What's it really saying, Julian?"

"Well, it's a love poem." Julian was a plausible but dim Etonian, one of four English students in Wynn's year, and her supervision partner for this term. "It's typical of Donne's metaphysical poetry. The first stanza is saying that they didn't really live until they loved, or that they were just children till then."

"Wynn, what do you think 'But sucked on country pleasures, childishly' in the third line might mean?"

"I suppose that they're linked, naively, by their closeness to nature and the divine creation; their love springs from that source, and though it's simple, it's as strong as the earth." Montagu looked unsatisfied, so she embellished. "But it might also mean something a little more physical, less elevated, like they took long walks, or maybe slept in hay barns or something?"

Montagu sniffed. "I don't think you're fully penetrating the imagery here. 'Sucked on country pleasures'." He split the salient word into two gendered sentences. "Cunt. Tree. Now do you see?"

Julian smirked, confirming Wynn's sense that she had erred not by insufficiently close reading but in lacking the puerility for this discussion. "Well, I thought I'd implied childish sexual play, but if we have to coarsely spell out the genitals to be sure we understand each other, fine."

She had feigned the outrage to fulfil Montagu's desire. Although she had not spotted that wordplay, it did not offend her. Academics, she learnt, were obsessed with finding in literature every vaginal cave, flower, chalice, spiral, and doorway, and every phallic spear, tower, obelisk, snake, and tree, all of which appeared to them as vast and ever-giving peepholes onto a refulgent tapestry of pudenda. But she also discovered that a humanities education taught her to unfurl the spiritual, psychological, and political mysteries of the poems, plays, and novels that she consumed prodigiously in libraries, from second-hand bookshops, and under her lovers' bookshelves as she lay in their beds on weekend mornings.

Wynn was practically alone in her wonder at the aesthetic sublime. She had hoped that university would be a different world from her childhood in Cornwall, with its constricted view of human possibility and cluelessness in the face of art. But even for supposedly elevated people like Montagu, Cambridge felt like it was all just punting and cunting.

"I'm sorry to say that Pearl has been rather unwell." Sister Maria, who ran the religious hospital, plucked a dead flower stem out of a cloudy glass vase in the hallway. "She had a bout of Covid, and then contracted some kind of syndrome, which I understand is exceedingly rare, and although the doctor hopes that she may make a full recovery in time, for the foreseeable future – and it is likely to be many months, I fear – she will be unable to use her hands. So one must be practical."

Wynn had brought a few of Pearl's pots, which had been fired at her uncle's workshop. She found Pearl sitting in her window overlooking the garden. Someone had provided a jug of homemade lemonade. Wynn lifted a glass to within Pearl's reach, so she could sip through a straw.

"Thank you, dear. I can't say how nice it is to see you. I'd give you a hug if it weren't for all this fuss, but I'm sure I'll be right when you come to visit next time."

Wynn's eyes moistened as she smiled. "I'm sure you will. I've brought your tenmoku vase and a few of your mugs. The glaze has come out beautifully, look: the black has broken so nicely to orange over the lip, and on those grasses you carved. I'm sorry; I should have brought you some flowers to put in it."

"Not to worry. Anyway, I'm hungry to hear all your news, so get cracking with your tales. And make sure they're full of wild young men, as I get nothing but nuns round here. They're very nice people, but low on sex appeal."

Wynn's first impressions of Julian seemed, in the end, to have been wrong. His world of giant houses and diplomat parents barely intersected with hers, but his wit and generosity had redeemed him sufficiently by the end of their degree that she and her boyfriend rented a flat with him in the outskirts of Cambridge.

Wynn had registered for a teaching qualification for the autumn, so that she could teach secondary-school English. Goodness knows what Julian did, but Ben had started working for a charitable foundation with offices in the city centre. Sometimes Wynn cycled in with him when he went to the office. She read Sebald in coffee shops all morning and wrote hopelessly ambitious imaginary lesson plans on his works in the afternoons.

One evening, when Ben was away, Wynn and Julian had sex on the couch. Sex was one of Julian's few undoubted skills, and although their fundamental incompatibility had from the start made all thoughts of a relationship a madness, their companionable erotics had played an important part in their friendship, even after Wynn got together with Ben. To her it had no effect on her relationship, but she was not confident that he would understand.

Julian was the only truly self-destructive person she knew. At least, that is how his drug-taking appeared to her: foolish, privileged, and blind to the indirect harm it did to the addicts who could not choose, as Julian could, when to stop using.

"You wouldn't feel so sour about it if you tried it," he said, as he Amexed white lines onto a tray.

The overdose, when it came, was both horrific and inevitable. But his hospitalisation was brief, and his family paid for him to spend six months in an upmarket rehabilitation spa in Gloucestershire. He did not return to their flat, and he did not pay his missing rent.

Three weeks after Julian's disappearance, Wynn took a bus to the hospital for her first ultrasound scan. She sat in an armchair and chatted to a surfer couple who were here for their second scan.

"Man, it's so epic seeing that little person lying there," said a radiantly happy young woman with skin that still looked unspoilt by puberty, let alone pregnancy, "and then they guess at their birthday for you. You're in for the most amazing day of your life."

The midwife called her in. An energetic woman with fingers like sausages. "Hello Wynn, my dear. How are you feeling? Have you been managing those pelvic floor exercises? You'll thank me for it in a few months, I promise!"

Wynn lifted herself onto the bed. "That's lovely – now let me see your tummy." The gel reminded her of slip, the slurry of thinned-out clay that she used to decorate serving platters with wavy designs not unlike the ones the probe was tracing on her belly. It felt lovely as it warmed. Wynn passed her eyes over the room. The midwife made a doubtful noise.

"I'm just going to check something again before I switch the monitor on."

Wynn began to feel unsettled. "Is there anything wrong?"

No amount of checking and re-checking could long delay the truth. There was no heartbeat. The foetus, her baby, had stopped growing two weeks ago. The midwife said something else, but Wynn did not hear. She sat in the waiting room for two hours. "No, there isn't anyone who can come for me – wait, yes, my boyfriend will have finished work. I'll give him a ring."

When Ben arrived, the midwife repeated Wynn's options. She would not wait. This must end now. She chose a vaginal pessary, and much earlier than they had hoped, her miscarriage started in the bus on the way home. Ben heaved her up two flights of stairs and into the bathroom.

The blood, though little more than a heavy period, seemed like an ocean in the water of the toilet, and Wynn hung faintly over her knees as Ben made phone calls in the living room. At some point something tiny but solid hit the ceramic bowl of the toilet, and Wynn shook with tears as she fished with blind hands for it in the black waters.

Years ago, she had checked her bum in the bar mirror before taking orders at the pub, but in the weeks that followed she avoided anything that could reflect her ravished body, with its enlarged, veiny breasts leaching away all their life-giving plumpness. They, it, and – when she made the mistake of stepping outside – the babies, the bellies, the mothers, the grandmothers, even those innocents who had not yet become pregnant, stalked and taunted her everywhere. She locked her staircase door, allowing only Ben inside, and smashed all her mirrors.

"I'm Pearl Treloar's nephew and am acting as her executor." Wynn, who had been lying foetally on the couch since her lunch three hours ago, lifted herself up on an elbow and held the phone to her other ear, enfolding her head in her hands. "As you know, she really enjoyed your visits to her at the home, and she had one or two items written by your name in her will. Is there a convenient time that you might be able to come and collect them?"

Ben brought them for her on the following afternoon. The bequest comprised a cushion that Wynn fancied she may have said she liked, and the tenmoku vase. It had been broken in seven pieces but had been given a *kintsugi* repair. Pearl must have loved it. Channels of gold lacquer trickled around the vase, inside and out, like rivers arrested by Midan hands while crossing a fertile black plain. One spidery line reached towards Pearl's carved patch of grass, lending a lustre of old gold to its deep orange-brown.

Ben bought her a bunch of spray carnations and Wynn set them in Pearl's vase, filling it with water from the tap. Having set it on their coffee table, she sat on the sofa and stood guard over it for quarter of an hour. She knew that *kintsugi* is not meant to make a pot usable again in its original form, but simply to preserve its fractured beauty as a reminder of the delicacy and transience, but also the dignified resilience, of life. Her vigil was therefore a nervous one.

But the vessel did not leak.

About the author
Paul Harper-Scott is the author of several non-fiction books on music. He grew up in the North East of England and now lives in Oxford. *A Tenmoku Vase* is his first piece of published fiction.

A Waste of a Life

Pete Pitman

As usual, it had been a long night. I was scared of the dark, but I daren't tell mum; she'd probably laugh at me. Now that weak sunlight had pushed back the fears, I began to think about the new day and this made my stomach gurgle with anticipation. It was an important day; I was on a mission.

I left for school ten minutes early to avoid my pals. Usually, I'd wait for Kosmo, my space mad friend, and together we'd walk up the street and call for roly-poly Pip. We went with Pip because his pockets were always stuffed full of snacks and sometimes he shared them.

I tip-toed past Pip's house, relieved his mother wasn't on sentry duty on her doorstep. She was the neighbourhood busy-body. I got up the street and around the corner without being seen, but in my rush almost stumbled over Inky, a barrel on legs with short, wiry, black hairs. The dog wandered the streets freely and was waiting for Pip. I raced past the big hall where the Sally Army band practised Sunday mornings. Past the bakery where you could buy yesterday's cream cakes for a penny. I skipped by the haberdashery shop with its Harry Worth windows. My heart was racing and not because I was out of breath.

I kept thinking, I hope he's there! I hope he's there!

I cut through the churchyard, which had a gate at each end, giving Pip two chances to distract Inky with a biscuit while we rushed through. Otherwise, the dog would follow him into school. Opposite the church was a big old derelict factory, a brooding monster with rows and rows of vandalised windows.

Pip had told us, "That used to be a Victorian workhouse. They reckon it's haunted!"

I wasn't sure what a workhouse was, but it sounded like a horrible place.

When we saw the bat sleeping upside-down beneath a top row windowsill, we all shouted, "It must be haunted."

I didn't like the workhouse; it seemed to draw my eyes through the shattered windows and deep into the horrific heart of the building. Everything was scaring me lately. I shuddered, before pulling away and running up the hill past the blue police box, just like the one in Dr Who. Kosmo was itching to get a look inside.

"Tardis," he said, the other week, "is Russian for 'travel machine'."

I knew it wasn't; he liked to make things up. He was mad about Yuri Gagarin, the Cosmonaut, and everything Russian.

I was almost there. My heart banged even more and my stomach went cold as I approached the waste paper factory. I don't know why it's called "waste", there's loads of brilliant stuff – bundles of empty cigarette packets, mounds of drawing paper, piles of coloured card, lots of beer mats, magazines, comics, and tons more.

I slowed down and leaned against the gate, afraid to enter. I thought about last week, when I'd sneaked in, looking for beer mats to skim at the girls as they left school. I was sorting through the best ones when a cab door opened and a lorry driver landed behind me. I nearly wet myself. I wanted to run, but my legs were like jelly.

The driver said, "You look like a good boy, do ya want some comics?"

"Y-yes, please," I said. And he gave me three Batman comics, two of which I hadn't read before.

"Behave yourself and ya can 'ave some more next week."

And now I was back. I'd lasted until Tuesday and couldn't

wait any longer. I'd come on my own because I didn't want to share them, especially with Pip.

I drew in a deep breath and tip-toed inside; the thought of free comics kept me going.

I was a long way from the safety of the gates, when one of the lorry drivers spotted me.

"Hoy!" he shouted.

I jumped two feet in the air and turned to run. I was about to high-tail it out of there when I recognised him as the bloke I was looking for. I gave him a big smile; I liked him.

"You're that good boy, who likes comics," he said. "Come over here. I'll see what I've got in mi cab."

He climbed into his lorry, looked down and said, "Do ya want to come and 'ave a look?"

"Y-yes, please."

He opened the passenger door and I clambered up inside. There was a big leather double seat covered in DC comics. My eyes nearly burst as they gobbled up this wonderful sight.

"Who d'ya like best then, sonny?" he asked.

"Superman and Batman, of course."

"Not Supergirl, then?"

"Not really, bit soft," I said, my eyes feasting on several I needed for my collection.

"Help yourself to a couple."

"Thanks, that's brilliant-y," I said, gently lifting up one Batman and one Superman comic.

"Do you like my lorry?" he asked.

"Yeah, it's really high up here. You can see loads."

"Well, if you come by Saturday morning, I'll take you out in the lorry on some deliveries. And we'll sort you out some comics when we get back."

"Th-that'd be sw-swinging," I said, my heart almost in my throat.

"But, don't tell anyone," he said, pressing his finger to his lips. "Am not s'posed to give them away. OK."

"I won't tell no one, honest."

The week dragged like a hundred school assemblies. Friday morning arrived with relief and the smell of cooking porridge and cigarette smoke. I'd had another bad night, imagining demons in the darkness beyond my bed. But, at last, it was almost the weekend. Only one more day left of school and then a trip in a lorry and free comics to look forward to. I'd never been in a moving lorry; I guessed it would be even better than sitting on the top deck at the front of the bus.

Kosmo was telling me about a refractor telescope he was getting for his birthday when we reached Pip's. Pip's mother was standing, floral pinny, matching scarf over her rollers, arms crossed, looking stern, on her doorstep.

"Hello, Mrs Reedman. Is Philip ready?" I asked. We daren't call him "Pip".

Pip appeared with a big smile and his chest puffed out. This was a bad sign; it meant somebody was going to suffer.

"Oh dear, look out!" said Kosmo.

"Did ya watch Z Cars, last night?" he said, knowing full well mum made me go to bed before it started. "It was swinging, yessirree."

He knew how to hurt me. Sometimes I wondered if it was worth putting up with him, just for the occasional snack bar or biscuit.

Kosmo talked to Pip about his telescope and I sauntered along behind them kicking at stones in the gutter.

Pip talked about Z Cars in a loud voice, "Yessirree, it was about football hooligans."

"Yeah, all right, Pip. So what?" I said.

But, he carried on. "This supporter thinks he's escaped this gang of football fans that's after him." Then more quietly to draw me in. "But, they're waiting for him in the entry to his terrace. Give him a right duffing."

By the time we reached the waste paper factory I was fuming so much, I couldn't resist saying, "I went in there on Tuesday. And the lorry driver gave me a load of comics."

"Never!" said Pip. "I want some."

"Well, tough!" I said, running off to school, wearing a big grin.

When I was alone in the playground, I remembered what the lorry driver said about not telling anyone. My eyes started to water and I ran to the toilets. Mum had said, "You never do anything right, do you?" And I was beginning to think she had a point. In the classroom, I sat at the back ignoring all my friends. I didn't want to let anybody else down.

Saturday morning arrived at last. I jumped out of bed at seven, my blood tingling. When I got downstairs mum was already there.

I was pouring some Corn Flakes into a bowl and thinking what a great day it was for a lorry ride, when she said, "Ah, I'm glad you're up. I need you to have a good wash and find your best shirt."

"W-why?" I asked.

"'Cus we're going to your Aunt Janet's for the day."

"N-no. We can't. I-I don't want to," I shouted, pushing my bowl across the table and slopping milk everywhere."

"You ungrateful little... so and so," she said, jumping up from her chair. "I sometimes wish I hadn't had..." She sat back down, pushed her hand through her hair and said, "You're going whether you want to or not."

I ran upstairs to my room just as my elder sister, Mary, was leaving her bedroom.

She tried to tickle me, but I pushed past her. She said, "Who's upset you, then?"

I mumbled, "Mum."

She gave me a sympathetic smile.

Mum had been a bit distant lately. I guessed it was because her sister, Janet, and Uncle Ron had plenty of money and were always going places and doing interesting things. Ron had a good job and they didn't have any kids, so they had a nice house and went on lots of holidays and trips.

Uncle Ron was all right; he was always telling jokes and he gave me and Mary five shillings each. Janet went on and on about all the things they owned and all the things they did. While she rambled on I thought about what the lorry driver would be thinking, now that I'd let him down. Another one! I decided the best thing would be to avoid him. The money from Uncle Ron would buy me a few comics.

When we got back, I got changed and went out to play football in the street.

"Where's Pip?" I asked Kosmo, while someone was climbing into a garden to fetch the ball.

"I dunno. He went off on his bike somewhere."

"That's OK," I said, having a dig back at Pip. "He's rubbish at football anyway."

That evening, I fell straight to sleep for the first time in ages, dreaming of dribbling past an entire team and scoring a goal at Wembley. I was woken by an insistent knocking at the front door. I thought I could hear shouts and hysterical sobbing, but it could have been the demons that were gathering in the gloom, ready to strike. After a while, someone over the road switched on a light which shone through the thin curtains and chased the demons away.

When I got up Sunday morning I knew instantly that something was wrong. It was quiet. None of the usual hustle and bustle – no radio blaring, no vegetables being peeled and no pots being washed. Mum sat at the table, red-eyed and tired looking, distractedly stubbing a half-finished cigarette into an already overfilled ashtray. Mrs Chapman, from next door, was just leaving.

"What's happened, Mum?" I asked.

Mum said, "I've got something to tell you; it's serious!"

I put down the Corn Flakes box I'd just picked up.

"Mrs Reedman came to see me last night. Young Philip went out on his bike in the afternoon and didn't come back."

"Yeah, Kosmo saw him go."

"Well, he still hasn't c-come home y-yet…" She started to cry.

I went all cold inside.

She regained control and continued, "…The police have been informed and your dad and some of the other fellas are out searching. Pl-please god, th-they find him well and safe."

So, it was Mrs Reedman I could hear last night.

Sunday afternoons were usually long and dull. This one was the worst ever – no television, not allowed to play outside and a constant stream of women came and went through the front room. I re-read some comics and thought about Pip. He wasn't that bad really; he liked to tease, but he usually gave you a Kit-Kat afterwards.

Monday morning, I ran downstairs and burst into a silent room. The previous day's events carouseled through my mind.

As I was eating my porridge, mum declared, "Mrs Chapman's nephew, Ben, will be walking you to school."

"Why?"

"Because I said so, all right!"

I met Kosmo and we ran to school struggling to keep pace with Ben's long legs. Inky made a half-hearted attempt to follow us, waddling away head bowed when Ben shooed him off. We arrived much earlier than usual. As the school yard filled up, the kids stood around in little groups, showing no interest in rolling marbles or kicking a ball. They found Philip Reedman's body that afternoon. School was cancelled the next day.

Wednesday, it was awful at home and at school. Nobody could concentrate and the teacher didn't even attempt to teach us anything.

They let us leave early, so me and Kosmo missed Mary who was supposed to meet us and bring us home. As we walked up past the police box, a man in a suit stepped out, followed by a policeman in uniform.

The be-suited copper shouted to us, "Hello boys, can we have a word with you?"

Kosmo got his wish, skipping happily inside with them, while I followed dragging my feet. It was nothing like the Tardis. It was hot, scary and cramped. The copper in uniform fiddled with his gloves, his helmet touching the roof, as the other one asked us strange questions about the driver at the waste paper factory.

"'As he ever tried to touch you?"

"No."

"No."

"'As he ever given you any money?"

"No."

"No."

"What about your pals? 'As he ever tried to touch them?"

"No."

"No."

We were both hot and frightened by this time, I'm sure they were deliberately scaring us.

"What sort of things does he say to you?"

Kosmo didn't know anything so he shut up and looked around.

"He doesn't; he just gives us comics," I told him, saying as little as possible because I wanted to get out of there.

"What sort of comics?"

"DC."

"What's DC?"

"You know, Superman and Batman!"

"All right, off you go; you've been lucky. In future, don't accept gifts from strangers, or talk to them, OK?"

Mary saw us coming out of the police box and walked us the rest of the way home.

She made me tell mum about my chat with the coppers.

When I'd finished, Mum burst into tears, pulled me close to her bosom and cried, "It could have been you!"

For a couple of seconds, I forgot all that had happened and it felt good having Mum hold me.

That night, I knew I wouldn't be afraid of the dark any more. I'd realised there was only one type of demon on this planet and one of them had devoured poor Philip Reedman.

About the author
Pete left school at fifteen and walked around the corner to work in the warehouse of a lace factory. He started writing on the bus to the Job Club, twenty years ago. He's had more than two dozen stories published in small presses and anthologies. Since retiring six years ago, he's written far less than he planned to.

Becoming Whole

Terry Sanville

"Too soon, too soon," Diane hissed through clenched teeth. The contractions hit hard, not helped by the bucking ambulance as it braked for the deep cross-gutters on Santa Barbara's West Side streets. Mitch held her hand; their fingers turned blue from her vice-like grip.

"We'll be there in a minute," Mitch said. "Just hang in there."

"Easy for you."

"I know, I know. Sorry."

It was their first pregnancy. They expected twins.

The ambulance lit up the quiet neighbourhood. But the EMTs didn't use the siren, no traffic at 3:30 AM. Family dogs slept, cats prowled, night-time irrigation systems did their job, and the baker rolled out of her bed to make breakfast before reporting to work. None took note of the all-too-common flashing drama that passed by.

At the hospital, Diane and Mitch entered the Birth Centre. Smiling nurses with dark patches under their eyes plugged her into various monitors. It had been a busy night.

"I'm scared," Diane admitted. "It's only been twenty-six weeks. They'll be too little."

"Don' worry, mama," Sylvia, a labour and delivery nurse said in a thick Southern accent. "We've got the best facility between LA and Frisco. We can handle anythin'."

Diane leaned back into the pillows and smiled, the smile changing into a grimace as the next contraction hit.

"They're eight minutes apart," Sylvia said. "But this is your first… so it could take a while."

"But they'll be so small."

"I know, darlin', I know. We have preemies born here all the time."

But Diane saw the worry behind the nurse's eyes as Sylvia watched the monitors, her smile pasted on, hands dancing across the computer keyboard on its portable stand. She finished verifying admissions information and sent off an electronic alert and phone message to Diane's obstetrician. Dr Sullivan arrived shortly thereafter, tried to hide her concern, her face wearing an optimist's mask.

The nurses and doctor left the couple alone, Diane having specified no epidural or other pain meds. They wanted their first to be born naturally with no drugs. They talked about rearranging their schedule, scrambling to finish the home nursery, letting their friends and family know about the births, and about how the first goal of their marriage, besides the wedding night, would soon be satisfied.

It took ten hours for twin girls to be born. The first one they named Ada after Diane's favourite aunt. Ada looked bluish and had a very low oxygen level for a newborn preemie. The nurses whisked her away. The second twin, Elise, came out pinker, and was named after Diane's favourite Beethoven piece. She too disappeared to the neonatal intensive care unit.

"When can I hold them?" Diane asked Sylvia.

"In a short while you can see them. But your girls will be in the NICU for some time until their lungs fully develop."

"How long will that be?"

"Near full term."

Diane felt her mouth drop open. "Two months?"

"Maybe less. But they need the time to develop."

Hours later the couple visited their daughters, looking

through the glass into the special care nursery where tiny Ada and Elise lay in incubators.

"I feel like I've failed," Diane said. "After all that work we're leaving this place empty-handed." Tears streaked her face.

"They're in good hands, honey," Mitch said. "And we can visit often until they're ready to come home. It'll give us more time to fix up the nursery and babyproof the house."

"Yeah, more time. If they'd just stayed inside me for a couple more months…"

Elise closed her book of crossword puzzles, the difficult version, and stared out the window at her twin sister Ada, playing in the backyard. Ada liked to swing and spent hours on the rusting swing set. Elise felt that day's first pang of envy and fingered the scars on her twelve-year-old chest. She'd had three heart surgeries with more to come as she grew. None of them had fixed her congenital heart problems.

Ada left the swings and chased the cat around the yard, a game that she loved dearly. Cio Cio San let her catch her and Ada filled her arms with the meowing Siamese and came inside.

"Cio Cio San slow," Ada said and laughed.

Elise grinned. "No she's not. You're just faster."

"Yes, I am. Mama says."

"Did you have fun swinging? It looks like you did."

"Yes. Fun."

Ada smiled and petted Cio Cio who purred loudly. She poured the cat out of her arms and sat next to Elise on the sofa.

"What that?"

Elise paused for a moment. "It's a game using words."

"Can I play?"

"No, not now, Ada."

Elise felt her heart thudding in her chest and breathed in long and slow. The pain gradually diminished. She stared at her identical twin. In the mirror across the room they looked like two yearling deer. Yet above Ada's perfect smile, her eyes stared blankly out, connected to the mind of a four-year-old. She would be forever young.

"Let's watch our favourite movie."

Ada grinned and settled into the sofa. Elise moved slowly toward the VCR and the shelf full of tapes. She pulled *The Wizard of Oz* from the collection and inserted it into the player. They watched the old movie starring Judy Garland.

"Do you girls want a snack?" their mother asked from the hallway. "It's two hours until dinner and Ada's been running around all day. I'm exhausted just watching her."

Elise grinned. "A snack would be great. How about crackers with peanut butter?"

Ada bounced up and down on the sofa. "Yes, yes, peanabuttar!"

"Coming up."

Ada quieted as the movie progressed. Elise almost cried when the Tin Man sang "If I only had a heart." She wiped her eyes on her sleeve when the Scarecrow sang "If I only had a brain." *That could be us in the movie*, Elise thought. *And we're just as pretty as Judy Garland. But neither of us are whole. Yet we're… connected.*

The following morning Elise awoke with a mild headache and lower stomach cramps. She peeled back the covers. Blood spotted her pyjamas and the sheet. She hurried to the bathroom. She and her mother had talked about periods and puberty several times and she knew what to do. The sanitary pads and tampons were kept under the sink where her father would never venture. She quickly dressed, her heart pounding too loudly, and went into the kitchen.

"Good morning, Sweet Cheeks," her mother said and kissed her on the forehead.

"I messed up the bed," Elise blurted.

"What's wrong?" Diane knelt before her and stared into her face.

"I got my period."

"I knew it would happen soon. You're been wearing that training bra for almost a year."

"Yeah, it sucks. Why do I have to wear it?"

"Just to help protect you as you mature."

"Yeah, yeah. Half the girls in my class are already falling out of their shirts."

"Don't worry, Elise. Growing up is not a competition."

"Wanna bet?"

Her mother sighed. "I'm more worried about Ada. How do I explain menstruation to your sister? She'll be scared."

"I'll help, Mama. I'll tell her it happened to me and that it's no big deal."

"Well it actually is. It was for me when I was your age."

"Did they even have birth control pills back then?"

"Oh, shush. It wasn't the Stone Age." Her mother's face coloured and she turned her back on Elise to fix breakfast.

Three days later Ada woke up crying. Elise helped her sister to the bathroom and showed her what to do. The adolescent four-year-old stood wide-eyed and shaking.

"It's okay, Ada," Elise said. "It happens to all girls growing up. It happened to me."

"Why?"

"When girls grow up they get breasts and have periods once a month. It's all part of maturing."

"I don' wanna mature."

42

Elise hugged Ada and eventually she stopped shaking. That night Ada came into her bed and they spooned. Elise tickled her and she giggled and begged her to stop. From then on, when the menses arrived each month, the twin girls would sleep together. Elise would make up fairy tales and whisper them to Ada until her sister fell fast asleep. They dreamed of handsome princes and beautiful maidens, in lands where no one got sick and everyone was smart as Einstein.

Elise felt weak when she awoke that morning. Rolling over in bed she grabbed her blood pressure cuff and took a reading – 91 over 74, the systolic a bit low. She figured it would come up once she got moving. She glanced over at Ada sleeping soundly in her bed. *She even smiles when she's asleep. I envy her, a day of swinging and chasing cats.*

She slowly dressed, the Catholic high school uniform fitting her snugly, a little girl's outfit to wrap a young woman's body. Her mom had fixed breakfast, a glass of OJ was all Elise would take. They sat in the morning sunlight and talked.

"What's going on at school today?" Diane asked.

"Same old sh—, er stuff," Elise said sleepily.

"Remember you've got that doctor's appointment right after school. So don't miss the van."

"I won't, m-o-t-h-e-r." She's so controlling. What's she gonna do when I leave for college? Poor Ada.

"Do you have your cell phone? Is it charged?"

"Yes, yes."

"Hey, you don't have to get mad. I'm just trying to make sure you're safe and—"

"I know, Mom. I get it."

"Is Janice coming to pick you up?"

"Yes."

43

"Good. I like that girl."

"I'm glad you approve."

Janice didn't really pick her up. She had a driver and they rode in the back seat of a Mercedes and talked about school and boys. Janice had matured as much as Elise and had gone on dates already, even though they had just turned sixteen.

"My mom won't let me date any boys," Elise complained.

"Why? Maybe you like girls better?"

"Cut it out. It's just that Mom thinks that if I get excited, like ya know, kissing or touching, I'll have a heart attack."

"That sucks."

"Yeah, tell me about it. I might as well sign up to become a nun."

"Not like Sister Agnus Saint Jude," Janice joked. "She thinks she's a general the way she orders us around."

At school the girls separated and went to different homerooms. Afterwards, Elise moved with care down the crowded school corridor, taking her time, not especially eager to get to her American Government class, a real snoozer. Mr. Abernathy droned on about the purpose of the Electoral College and how it came about. Soft yawns punctuated his lecture.

Elise felt her cell phone vibrate and she checked her texts. A new one from her mother read, "We have a medical emergency. Your father will be outside the school to pick you up. I have notified the principal."

Right in the middle of Mr. Abernathy's argument for why we should graduate from the Electoral College, Elise stood and moved toward the door.

"Where are you going, Elise?" the teacher asked.

"Medical emergency." She held up her cell phone.

"All right. But check at the principal's office before you leave campus."

Elise ignored his comment and moved directly to the main entrance and out. Her father had just pulled their Toyota to the curb and she climbed in, her heart thudding away, face hot.

"What's going on?"

"Your sister has had some kind of stroke. They want all of us to come to the Emergency Department. We'll get the full story there."

Elise stared at her father, his face pale, lips trembling. She could tell he held back something important but didn't press him. He already drove too fast and she cinched her seatbelt tight and tried to control her breathing.

Elise's mother and two doctors met them outside Room 4 in the hospital's Emergency Department. Tears dripped from her mother's dark eyes, staring out from a ghostly face. Curtains had been pulled across the window that looked into Ada's room.

"What's going on, Mom? What's happened to Ada? Is she all right? Can I see her?"

Diane and the doctors looked at each other. Then her mom spoke. "Your sister was playing on the swings and had a stroke. She... she died."

Elise felt her throat close up and she gulped for air. "What? How? I don't understand..."

One of the doctors spoke. "She had a brain aneurysm. It burst and there was a major brain bleed. Nothing could be done. But we have her on a heart-lung machine that's keeping her, well, alive, technically."

"Can I see her?" Elise asked.

The doctor nodded and a nurse entered Ada's room and drew back the curtains. Ada lay on the bed, looking as if asleep, a smile creasing her pretty face. Elise choked back a sob.

"She... she looks alive."

The second doctor spoke. "Yes, she does. Except for the aneurysm, she's in amazingly good shape."

"Why are you telling me all this? She's dead. My... my beautiful twin sister is dead." Elise sobbed loudly and her mother hugged her, the two shaking in their grief.

The doctors waited until they calmed somewhat.

"The reason why we're telling you," one doctor said, "is that your sister's heart is in perfect condition. We know that yours is not. With your support and your parents' consent we want to transplant her heart into you. I know this is a lot to take in, but we need to know now and prep you for surgery."

"I would have my sister's heart?"

"Yes, since you are identical twins, it will be a perfect match. And you probably won't need to take anti-rejection drugs."

Elise's mother stepped forward. "Elise, honey. I know this is happening so fast. But part of Ada could survive in you and you could become... whole. No more complaints from the Tin Man. With every beat of Ada's heart she will be with you and with us."

Within two hours, Elise lay on the operating table, her chest exposed. The anaesthesiologist placed a mask over her face and told her to breathe deeply. She slipped into dreamland where she and Ada skipped happily down the yellow brick road, heading for Oz, with the Tin Man, Scarecrow, and the Cowardly Lion trailing behind.

When Elise got married to Harry, she petitioned to change her last name to his and her middle name to Ada. And later, as her daughter grew into a beautiful little girl, she installed a swing set in their back yard. Mother, daughter and Ada would talk and swing. The little girl took to it naturally, and

Elise enjoyed it more and more with every beat of their heart.

About the author
Terry Sanville lives in San Luis Obispo, California with his artist-poet wife (his in-house editor) and two plump cats (his in-house critics). He writes full time, producing short stories, essays and novels. His short stories have been accepted more than 500 times by journals, magazines, and anthologies including *The American Writers Review*, *The Bryant Literary Review*, and *Shenandoah*. He was nominated three times for Pushcart Prizes and once for inclusion in *Best of the Net* anthology. Terry is a retired urban planner and an accomplished jazz and blues guitarist – who once played with a symphony orchestra backing up jazz legend George Shearing.

Deferred

Hamid Harasani

I spend my mornings staring at dead people.

They stare back; some smiling, some serious, some expressionless.

My ancestors.

Up on the wall opposite my desk, just by the rickety bookcase stacked with old medical journals, is my great grandfather, angry and bitter. To his right, past the entrance, is my grandfather, my Jiddo, smiling while shying away from the camera. Both long dead, yet alive with me all morning, every morning.

The call had been made to my uncle a few weeks back. A family meeting had been convened. I was tasked by my father to prepare my Jiddo's majlis, as his home had been uninhabited since his death. The majlis was left as it had always been in my Jiddo's life, partially shelved with various books, a large picture of the Kaaba's golden door opposite where he normally sat, classical sofas and armchairs, and a massive Persian rug to cover the marble floor.

Amongst the many roles my father asked of me, I served as an unofficial secretary to the beneficiaries of my Jiddo's estate, namely my two uncles, two aunts, and my father. I wouldn't always attend their meetings but would be solely responsible for executing any action points, as communicated to me by my father. *Sell this land, make this bank transfer, or donate to that charity.* All the beneficiaries trusted me, and only me, and I was therefore the only person with a wide-ranging power of attorney from all of them.

That evening, my father asked me to wait outside as they met. I sat for an hour and a half jumping from one phone app to another: responding to messages, browsing social media, or reading political articles. Just as my phone's battery was close to dying, my aunt Salma walked out of the room, her maroon kaftan glistening under the hallway spotlights.

"You'll have your work cut out for you this time," she said, before pecking my cheek and leaving, the floral aroma of her perfume lingering for a little while longer.

I bid everyone else farewell, then joined my father in the majlis. He was sitting where my Jiddo always sat. With receding grey hair, strong eyes, and a young face that betrayed his age, the resemblance he had to my Jiddo was remarkable. Yet he could not be more different in mannerisms and actions. My Jiddo, a poet amongst many things, had a deep passion for literature and learning, while Father barely read the morning newspaper. My Jiddo was glued to Makkah, while Father was a serial traveller. My Jiddo was a man of tradition while Father embraced modernity. They were opposites in almost everything except for their devotion to family.

A commotion lifted from the main road outside; the noisy rattle of a bus coming to a halt, the boom of a voice from a megaphone charging out instructions, and the hustle and bustle of pilgrims walking in file along the narrow pavement adjacent to my Jiddo's house. The pilgrims headed to one of the many high-rise hotels that had sprung up in the place of the demolished house in our neighbourhood in the last decade; a quiet residential area had been transformed into an accommodation hotspot for thousands of worshipers that incessantly flocked to Makkah. Hajj was less than a month away; a city of two million would more than double in size.

After some contemplation, my father finally looked up at me. "Your uncle Faisal received a call from a government official about sequestering one of our lands in Makkah. The land they described, in Jabal Omar, is not on our asset list. I just double checked with your uncles and aunts; none of them know of it."

I was a little taken aback by the notion that both my Jiddo and father may have missed itemising a piece of property. I had never thought one of them capable of such an error, let alone both. Both, if this mistake is indeed a mistake, are fallible after all. I looked up at my father and could see the disappointment in his face, the look of someone who was livid with himself for committing an error or overseeing something important.

My father never had to be motivated or inspired; perfectionism was an inner beast that dwelled within him, reproaching him at each lapse or minor slip. His internal battles and struggles could only be read by those who understood the subtle signs disclosed by his face: slight frown, furrowed eyebrows, failure to make eye-contact. That would be the extent of it. No apologies, excuses, or admissions. The dejection that I was sure he felt inside was overcome by the pride he always maintained on the outside. As such, I was mindful not to say anything, for the best solutions in his eyes were those he proposed.

"You need to go to the basement and sift through the archives," he said. "It may take hours if you're very lucky. But I expect it will take days, or weeks. All we know is that the land is in Jabal Omar. Until the call came, I didn't know of any lands your grandfather owned there. You will search every file, inspect every document."

"Of course."

My father picked up his mobile and rang his driver, a signal that our brief meeting was over. As always, my father was a big picture person who would instruct one to go from A to B, leaving that person to figure how to execute or bring about his instruction. The implementing regulations were all left to me – I just had to get things done. He hated being asked "how", "why", or "what", but tolerated "when". What if I can't find anything? A question I dared not ask but could do little to prevent myself pondering upon.

And so, my task began.

The tactful review of thousands of foxing documents. I would collect several files at each visit, and take them up to my Jiddo's antique desk, and go through them under the stares of my ancestors from their portraits opposite me. I spent four hours each day, which was all I could spare. I would pray Fajr near my Jiddo's house and commence work on the documents from around 6 am. Assisting me was Ali, my Jiddo's ancient servant who hailed from Kerala.

Ali was a scrawny, dark-skinned old man well into his seventies. He always wore a white Thob, with its sleeves rolled up to his elbows, eager to get cracking on whatever task he was asked. My Jiddo had adored him, and Ali was a faithful servant to him until his last breath. And after my Jiddo's death, Ali wailed louder than everyone else, sincerely lamenting his loss, making us all feel like it was the end of the world.

Weeks afterwards, my father offered to send Ali back home with a generous monthly pension for life, but Ali refused. Home is Makkah, he would say. Ali held my Jiddo's manner of death in awe, forsaking home, family, and rest in the silent hope and prayer that he too could be taken in the Sacred City. And so, and out of revere and appreciation, the family kept him in his post: a servant in a mansion that had no inhabitants.

Though he only spoke broken Arabic, Ali was the

caretaker of my Jiddo's archives. He had itemised all files and documents diligently. My Jiddo was an organised man, and he had overseen Ali's work in cataloguing files and documents by year. The oldest documents were records of Hajj expenses in the 1920s, the time when the Sharif Hussein ruled Makkah. Written with faded ink, there were tables and tables of expenses, which I could not really make much sense of. At the end of each account, I could see my great grandfather's signature and ring stamp.

"This is gold," I said to Ali. "It needs to be restored and well kept! The termites will eventually nibble at it, and damage it completely in that damp basement."

"There are no termites under my watch." Ali frowned.

"Of course not, Ali. I didn't mean it that way."

Ali shrugged and went about his chores.

As the file years progressed, I began to see markings of my Jiddo. His chronicles of expenses, a type-written table which must have been seen as a big leap towards modernisation back in the 1950s. Later, I saw letters written by my uncles, aunts, and father to my Jiddo. Children's letters, though written with much more eloquence and formality than any child glued to his iPad could write today. They address my Jiddo back then like we would address a minister or a prince today. All the letters commenced with exaltations of respect and deference, making enquiries about all senior family members alive then. My Jiddo's response letters to them were nowhere to be found, as he probably didn't keep copies of what he wrote back, and I very much doubted that my father, aunts and uncles had copies of their childhood correspondences with their father.

My Jiddo, however, did keep copies of all the important letters he wrote. Letters to ministers, foreign dignitaries, and one or two letters to the ruling king at the time. And how beautifully did my Jiddo write. Outstanding penmanship, and a deep command of language or vocabulary. *"It is this valley that Allah has exalted above all valleys. Not for its trees, for it is baren, nor for its rivers, for it is dry; for the sprinkle of sacredness that touches its farthest corners. Makkah, where even the mightiest of men shrink before the grandiosity and majesty that is the Kaaba,"* he wrote in one letter addressed to the Ambassador of Egypt.

With each review of a document, I sensed I was peeling another layer and diving deeper into my Jiddo's life: letters to his wife, my late grandmother, theories about society which were written for his own eyes only, and deeply passionate appeals to senior officials on many issues he deemed important. All written by his hand and concluded with his signature which oddly resembled a pirate ship. He had intended for everything archived to be stumbled upon. *He must have.* And if so, then there must be many documents that he destroyed, deeming them too private, or unsuitable for viewing by anyone else, ever. I wondered how many of these documents there were.

There were of course many documents pertaining to land acquisitions or sales he made in Makkah, Taif, and Jeddah. Weeks into my research and I could not find a single document about land in Jabal Omar, but there were still four decades of archives left to review, and I was still hopeful that I would find something.

When I reached a file marked *"1980: the dreadful year"*, my Jiddo's sentiment, as deduced by his writings, had transformed like nothing I had seen. The first document in the file was an undated, unaddressed, untitled note.

"Sorrow has thrust its sharpest of daggers straight into my heart. With every waking moment, I ache all over. Sleep eludes me. The love of my life, my breath of fresh air, my everything has passed away to the mercy of Allah. I accept her fate, and that I must, but I cannot bear the pain," the

53

note commenced, and went on for a page and a half, an exposé on deep melancholy and grief.

I always knew that my grandmother's death had deeply pained my Jiddo. The extent of his agony only became apparent as I read his writings. Up until his last days, he would remember her and a tear or two would streak down his wrinkled cheeks, followed with murmured prayers to Allah for her soul and salvation. She died a few months before I was born, and my mother had always told me how my birth had brought a smile to my Jiddo's face. She had spoken of how he had carried me, called the Athan in my right ear and the Iqama in my left, performed *Tahnik* on my lips, and pronounced my name for the first time, Ahmad. You gave him much solace, she would say.

When Ali walked in carrying a steel pot of sweetened mint-tea that morning, I asked him to fetch another cup and join me. He nodded and returned with a glass teacup. Ali sat in the chair opposite, and I poured us both some tea.

"How long have you been here, Ali?"

"It is 2005 today, so it has been thirty-five years."

"So, you remember my grandmother?"

"Very much so, of course. She was a very kind woman. Pious. Very pious."

"It appears from the files that my Jiddo found it difficult to bear her death."

"It was… we all found it difficult. It was so sudden, and she was so young. She slept one night and decided not to wake up."

I had to keep ploughing through the files. Other than the traumatic death of my grandmother, the early 1980s were dull and uneventful. My father, uncles, and aunts had all grown up by then. My Jiddo had retired, his many vocations were mostly relinquished. The documents I worked through were records, bills, and lease contracts.

With the advent of the 90s the trail revealed the

discomforts my Jiddo must have suffered as he lived his declining years. Medical report after medical report: heart problems, diabetes, hypertension, amongst many other ailments. No letters, financial reports, or political writings; my Jiddo, it seems, had by then been pushed to the farthest periphery of life, the waiting room for the afterlife. As I went through the files, I remembered him sitting in his armchair lost in deep silence. On the days his melancholy gripped him most, he would be vocal about his desire to join his wife in Al-Muallaa cemetery. "How I long for the re-union?" he would say. He would fantasise about being walked to his resting place like a bride being walked to her groom.

As I completed my review of the 90s files, I felt an overwhelming sense of sorrow and sadness. The files had not revealed anything I had not seen myself, but they had made me re-live moments I had almost forgotten. When I remembered my Jiddo, I always selectively reminisced on our most colourful memories: Eid breakfast, his literature evenings hosting Makkah's greatest poets, and the stories he told us when we were younger about his childhood in a Makkah that was very different from the one I grew up in. That is how I chose to remember him, that is how I wanted to remember him.

My phone rang shortly after I wrapped up my careful inspection of the 90s files. I was driving back home. It was Father.

"Salam Alaykom, Ahmad."

"Wa Alaykom Alsalam, Father."

"You can stop working on the archives now. We found what we needed."

Just like that, months of work and going through hundreds of documents had been halted. Though I was relieved that my father found what he was looking for, I was disappointed that it had not been found by me. I was also dismayed that my daily routine, imbedding a surreal sensation that my Jiddo was by my side, would come to an end. He spoke to me via his many documents and little did I imagine how much I longed for that voice, how I was attached to it.

"Where did you find it?"

"Your uncle Faisal found it in the safe at the bank buried under a stack of documents. A clear land deed."

So, my Jiddo had not made a mistake, he did not omit any documents his beneficiaries would need to distribute his estate. It was everyone else's fault but his.

"Understood. Thank you, Father. If there is anything else I can do, please let me know."

He coldly thanked me and hung up. I decided to take a detour and made my way to Alhujoon Road. As I drove, I could hear Thuhur prayer being called from the various mosques that were nearby. It was a scorching day. My windscreen was searing under the sun, and I could feel the oppressive heat on my face. The temperature in my car registered 49 degrees Celsius. Noon was not a pleasant time to be driving in Makkah. Nonetheless, I felt like I had to go where I was heading, like I had little choice.

Al-Muallaa is an ancient burial ground, engulfed between mountains on three sides. Khadija, Prophet Mohamed's first wife, was buried there alongside her eldest son Qasim over 1,400 years ago. The graves in Al-Muallaa are marked by nothing more than a massive rock for each male, and two smaller rocks for each female. Each row of graves is numbered, and clusters of graves walled by short white enclosures are scattered across the hilly terrain. There are no tombstones, names, dates, or flowers; a place as devoid of life as the desert is devoid of water. Some mourning relatives would scatter pigeon feed above the graves of their loved ones, and the pigeons of Makkah would first swarm above, then flock to feed there in their tens or hundreds.

Al-Muallaa's gates are opened after each prayer for fresh burials, and that would be an opportunity for people like me to enter and visit their buried loved ones. I prayed nearby and arrived just before the latest coffins arrived from the Kaaba Mosque. As I walked into the cemetery, a wave of simoom had taken grip, and each breath suffocated and burned my nasal cavity.

"Water?" I heard a man call behind me. I turned around to find a bare-headed elderly man, his hand extended towards me with an ice-cold bottle of water. "Cool yourself down, son. Take it."

I took it, thanked him, and he walked away towards a different area of the cemetery. The gulps of cold water moistening my mouth and throat were bliss, and it somehow made the oppressive heat and beating sun that little bit more bearable. Armed with my shades and Shumagh to cover my head, I walked up the hilliest part of the Al-Muallaa towards my Jiddo's resting place. The minarets of the Kaaba Mosque could be seen from where he was buried.

When I finally arrived at my Jiddo's grave, I found myself panting heavily. Sweat had drenched my inner garments. I was alone in that section of the cemetery, the only living soul standing amidst hundreds of graves. I crouched down by my Jiddo's grave and made the usual prayers and supplications for Allah to show him mercy and grant him His everlasting bounty. I then sat silently, alternating my glances between the Kaaba Mosque in the horizon, and my Jiddo's grave just below my feet.

"Even after you have long parted, you continue to shower us with your kindness, Jiddo," I said, then paused to wipe the sweat that had formed across my forehead. "My baba has found Jabal Omar's deed. I don't know if you intentionally kept it out of initial reach. Nonetheless, Jiddo, it has been found now. I just wanted to let you know."

With that off my chest, I made my way to the exit. I walked past the arriving new coffins, mourning relatives, and tens of visitors that had by then started to enter the cemetery. As I drove back home, revitalized by the cool air emitted from my car's air-conditioning, I asked myself the same question over and over. *Did he hear me? Did he hear me?*

About the author

Hamid Harasani is a Saudi lawyer, resident in Jeddah, Saudi Arabia. With a PhD in law from King's College London, he is an accomplished and published legal researcher. He believes in creative writing as a means to introduce and understand different cultures; to reduce culture clashes, tensions, and to foster coexistence. Hamid's short story *When the Rain Stops* has won the Yeovil Prize for writing without restrictions in 2023.

Desperately Seeking Talent

Allison Symes

"What, again? What did Michelle bring down this time?"

"Just the kitchen ceiling, boss."

"What was Michelle doing – magic, cooking, or both?"

"Just cooking, boss."

"What on earth was she trying to make?"

"A soufflé, boss."

"I know they're meant to be light and to rise but I've never heard of one bringing the ceiling down before."

"That happened when Michelle threw her finished baking at the ceiling, boss."

"I suppose we should be grateful she didn't decide to throw it at someone."

"Indeed, boss. One positive thing is the other Year 1 students have stopped laughing at her now. They're looking considerably more wary. That's probably a good thing."

"I suppose I should see the wretched girl. What would you recommend, Hamley?"

"Full body armour, boss. Don't stand too close to a window. Keep half an eye out on your own ceiling, boss. Just check you have got your life insurance premiums up to date before you call her in."

"Very good, Hamley. Can you ask Michelle to come and see me in half an hour? That should give enough time for my relaxation pills to kick in."

"You are aware this is a college for gifted students, Michelle?"

"I don't mean to be so clumsy, boss. I really don't know how it happens. And I'd hoped that focusing on one thing at a time rather than trying to combine magic with cooking would've meant I improved but…"

"I know, I know. And you do have talent. You passed your exams with flying colours. You have a gift for friendship few share and that has been appreciated by all. You also seem to have a talent for making people laugh."

"Yes, by being clumsy, boss. It does nothing for my morale. I don't want to go down that route. If I wanted to be a clown, I would've joined the circus, not come to a magical college."

"I think I have an idea. I can think of a number of students here who do well with course work but struggle with exams. You seem to take exams in your stride. Do you think you could assist them?"

"I could try, boss. At least I wouldn't be bringing down another wretched ceiling!"

"Okay, Hamley, I can see you peering around the door. What has Michelle wrecked this time? Do we need to get the plasterers in again?"

"No, boss. We do need to get in fresh lots of ink and paper. When she tried to help the students with their exam prep, the ink wells exploded. Before you ask, I did check and our more mischievous students have not done anything here. That girl is pure bad luck on legs."

"There must be something we can do with that to use it to our advantage. It is a gift of a sort."

"Yes, boss, to our enemies. They would love to see the damage Michelle is doing."

"Now there's a thought."

"Boss, really! Please, no."

"Keep calm, Hamley. We show them what Michelle can do and threaten to set her loose on them if they don't leave us alone. That's got to be worth a go, surely?"

"So I am to take this letter of yours to the Elderians, boss? The beings that hate us? The beings that deliberately dump their rubbish all over our planet to show the rest of the universe what they think of us?"

"The very same, Michelle. You go tomorrow and by first class shuttle too with loads of lovely refreshments, including your favourite cakes and drinks. Enjoy yourself."

"But I'm no good at diplomacy."

"I suspect it's not diplomacy the Elderians need."

"They will let me come back here, won't they, boss?"

"I suspect they'll be eager to see you on your way back here again in no time, Michelle. I am usually right on these things. I have a highly developed gut instinct. Never lets me down."

"You've said something in that letter, haven't you, boss?"

"It's better you don't know the letter's contents, Michelle. It means you can genuinely tell the Elderians you don't know. They value truth telling. Just a pity they don't value us or the idea of dealing with their own rubbish rather than dumping it elsewhere. Anyway, do see this as an invaluable learning experience. I am sure many lessons will be learned and not just by you."

"That's your gut instinct talking again, boss, yes?"

"Oh yes, Michelle. As I said, it never lets me down. I like to think of it as my own special little gift and where I can use it in the service of our people, even better."

"Okay, boss, I admit it. I was wrong. Those peace negotiations were hugely successful and we're not going to be bothered by the likes of the Elderians again."

"All we have to do is keep Michelle away from them."

"I heard she managed to destroy three major roads, a super shop, and the Parliament building just by pointing her wand the wrong way. But it was when she managed to crash their entire world's internet and traffic systems, they

61

begged for mercy. They couldn't get her back to us quickly enough once their engineers had got their transportation up and running again. I guess Michelle does have a kind of talent, boss."

"Do we tell Michelle she's gifted in an unusual way do you think, Hamley?"

"I wouldn't, boss. It might put her off her stride! Anyway, she doesn't want to be a clown, remember? But we need to do something to cheer her up a bit. While we were delighted the Elderians were only too eager to have peace talks with us after over a century of hostility thanks to unleashing Michelle on them, I don't think the girl herself was too happy about how it came about. We need to find her a role she could do which is clearly useful."

"Call her in, Hamley. I think I have the very role for her."

"Really?"

"Oh yes. She can be my personal assistant, answerable to you and to me. We will deploy her as and when we see fit. When on duty, well she loves a good read. She can't do any harm in a library, especially if we insist she leaves her wand outside. And we can tell her it's all for research purposes. Some it may well end up becoming so given I can think of a few neighbouring worlds we could do with keeping an eye on. The Elderians aren't the only pains in the universe."

"You wouldn't, boss…"

"Wouldn't what, Hamley?"

"Send her to Earth? Please, for the love of all that is sacred, no."

"Have no fears there, Hamley. Earth has enough of its own gifted people talented enough to muck up their planet. They don't need us or Michelle interfering."

"Oh good. Did you want me to square things with our

librarian, boss? She ought to be prepared for Michelle spending a lot of time in her domain."

"True. She might want to reinforce the ceiling for a start. Yes, please, Hamley, the sooner the better. And then send Michelle in. I'm sure she'll be pleased."

"And it is okay with the librarian?" Michelle looked nervously at the older woman who was taking care to stand as far away from the girl as it was possible to get in the boss's office.

"It is fine, Michelle. Certain amendments have been made…"

"You've reinforced the ceiling, haven't you, boss?"

"Of course, Michelle. Didn't want anything untoward disturbing your reading, did we? Now off you go with the librarian. I want you to look up some histories for me. It will take you a while. Happy reading."

"That was one way to sweeten things for the librarian, boss," Hamley said once the visitors had gone. "Send Michelle down to the vaults for the history files. I do hope she's not scared of the dark. They've never been able to get enough lighting there. Even magical lighting doesn't seem to 'take' down there."

"I suspect Michelle will manage just fine. And so will we. The ceiling down there is reinforced. The area is fire-proofed, water-proofed, and every other kind of proofed you can imagine. As for whether it's Michelle-proofed, time will tell."

"What, again? What did Michelle bring down this time? She can't have done anything in the library vaults surely, Hamley?"

Hamley grinned. It had been lovely watching the panic-stricken expression on his boss's face the moment he peered around the office door again. The last time had been over six months ago. It had been quiet, maybe a little too much so. "All is well, boss, but we do have another problem to contend with and it isn't Michelle."

"Good. That's a relief so what is it then?"

"The rats who lived down in the cellar, note the past tense, boss, want union representation. Michelle told them the story of that guy and the odd business in Hamelin. Goodness knows why but she did. The rats say they're not going anywhere with anyone unless there's a decent amount of cheese in it for them. It appears Michelle has a gift for storytelling too. Any thoughts, boss?"

About the author:
Allison Symes is a flash fiction/short story writer, blogger and editor. She runs writing workshops, judges competitions, and writes weekly for writers for *Chandler's Ford Today*. Allison has two flash fiction collections published (Chapeltown Books) and has short stories in various anthologies. She is an editor for an online magazine.

Flowers for She Who Wants to See Them

Zoe Stanton-Savitz

Adeline St. James dragged a single gloved finger through the blood oozing from cold flesh. She lifted her pinky, now dotted with a drying red droplet, to her nose. She couldn't resist the familiar scent, putrid and metallic, only a few hours old. Carefully, and with a steady hand, Adeline pressed her scalpel into the blue-ish skin at the slope of the shoulder and tugged it diagonally to the bottom of the sternum. Fresh blood seeped from the incision and clung to the sleeves of her lab coat.

The man who lay before her on the plastic-covered coronary stretcher had three stab wounds in the centre of his protruding stomach. Though the serrated edges implied a murder or suicide – the culprit, judging by the size and shape, a kitchen steak knife – Adeline wanted to fully understand the circumstances in which this man had died. Perhaps he was a drinker, for example, which might indicate depression or erratic behaviour or perhaps the stabbing occurred after his heart had already stopped, and the wounds only artifice disguising the true crime. Every detail must be considered.

She began to remove the organs, slowly and methodically examining the intricate detailing in each vein, tendon, and muscle, like an art critic scrutinizing even the most minute brushstrokes in an oil painting. Although this was probably about the two-hundredth body she had examined, Adeline always marvelled at the individuality of each cadaver – the unique branching patterns of veins, the distinct collage of varying reds and purples within a body, the serenity of each ashen, lifeless, face.

First the heart. It glistened a deep rosewood hue beneath

the lab's fluorescent lighting. Slightly enlarged, Adeline noted. Perhaps a heart attack. Or maybe just high blood pressure. She placed it in a metal tray to her left, and moved on to the lungs. She continued this way for a few moments, noting not only imperfections, but also revelling in the artistry, the particularness and specificity of this human body.

She noticed the intricacies in each organ: the way the trachea branched down into the lungs like the roots of a young tree, the way the spots on the liver created a dappled pattern, the way the small intestine coiled perfectly beneath the stomach.

Something caught Adeline's eye. Wedged into one of the stab wounds was a blood-soaked slip of paper, folded methodically. She gingerly pulled it out and, unfolding it slowly, held it to the light to decipher the words smudged in black ink. Though it was scrawled messily and splattered with blood, Adeline could easily make out two words in familiar handwriting: "Hi Addie."

Adeline had always been solitary. She had grown up curious, enamoured with the mangled bodies of skunks and squirrels at the side of the road: contorted necks, matted fur, lacerated skin revealing the pinkish goo of ravaged innards.

As a child, Adeline walked a mile to her school from her family's Nebraska farmhouse, shielded by a canopy of oak trees, along the road where these unsuspecting creatures skittered, invisible to drivers. She knelt beside the animals and looked into their cold inanimate eyes, wondering what their last thoughts had been. The habit sparked her interest in the dead and dying, an interest that rendered her "Creepy Addie" to schoolmates and bought her a trip to the local shrink.

Adeline was crafty with her words, though, and able to subdue any worry about her sanity by attributing her obsession with roadkill to an interest in simple biology. The nickname, however, followed her into young adulthood and Adeline isolated herself from those with working minds and hearts. They were too unpredictable and ever-consumed by emotions that Adeline, despite her attempts to understand, found most confounding.

The only time when Adeline thought she might understand the land of the living, when she felt something akin to love, had been with Fiona.

Unsurprised by the note, Adeline finished the examination and turned to the report. From her coat pocket she removed a pen and under "Medical Examiner" she jotted her own name. Then, she wrote "possible suicide or murder. No foreign DNA or unusual markings. Three stab wounds in lower abdomen, unhealthy liver, enlarged heart. Cause of death…" Adeline's pen hovered. She bit her bottom lip. She scratched her nose. "Cause of death: exsanguination."

Then, Adeline removed her gloves. She fished into her bag, which hung on a hook by the entrance to the lab, and retrieved a lanyard of keys. Accompanying a plastic dinosaur keychain were her car keys, a key to her apartment, one to her mailbox, one to the lab, and an indistinct little silver one. With this, Adeline opened a lockbox that was hidden in the corner of the lab between an industrial-sized sink and a tower of metal drawers in which body parts were sometimes stored if they had particular pertinence to a case.

Adeline rifled through the collection of newspaper clippings and trinkets kept in the box for the umpteenth time, reading the familiar headlines: *"$800,000 yacht belonging to Judge Robert Mcintyre set aflame following contentious ruling," "Mcintyre found dead after ruling against seventeen-year-old Mia DeMarco," "Judge Mcintyre's failure to punish sexual assault assailant leads to arson attack."*

From the box, Adeline tenderly lifted the shard of deck wood with an engraved heart that had been left at the scene of the crime. Placing it back in the box, Adeline sifted through the next stack of clippings: *"California representative presumed murdered after controversial Tweet,"*, *"Rep. Catherine Hartley bans books for 'glorifying the homosexual agenda' "*, *"Arsenic found in representative Hartley's bloodstream two days following her book banning"*. One of the clippings showed a picture of the corpse's white face, a daisy tucked behind its ear. Adeline found that same daisy in the lockbox, now dried and brown; she dared not pick it up for fear the petals would crumble with her touch.

After the first one, Adeline realized Fiona's game. She was leaving Adeline clues, keeping herself tethered in her own scheming way. And Adeline relished these gifts as reminders of Fiona's love.

Adeline worshiped Fiona's honey-brown eyes, knowing that something fiery burned behind their kindness.

She had tried to rationalize her feelings for Fiona; it was only hormones, just the brain releasing oxytocin from physical affection. But it was hard to rationalize the feeling of warmth and complete assurance she felt when she gazed at Fiona's innocent face: doughy and round, with freckles splattered across her nose and a rosy glow painting her cheeks.

Fiona, the girl with the wild raven hair, barely five feet tall, who had picked Adeline from a crowd of infinitely more interesting and beautiful girls, would say the two were twin flames – one soul separated into two bodies. She believed in all the supernatural nonsense that Adeline scoffed at – Adeline was, after all, a woman of science.

"We're sister signs, you know," Fiona had said once, Adeline entangled in her arms in the bed that had been theirs. "You're an Aquarius. I'm a Leo."

"What does that even mean?" Adeline asked.

"It means you're smart," she said, kissing Adeline's forehead. "And independent," kissing her cheek. "And you spend a lot of time in your own head," kissing her neck.

"And you," Adeline whispered, losing her breath.

"I'm fiery."

Adeline forced a smile through the gloom that invariably struck at the thought of Fiona.

Now, the bed they had shared was Adeline's alone. Fiona had vanished, the only clue a yellow daisy left on Adeline's pillow. Adeline had sent seventeen never-delivered texts and when she tried to call, she received only an error message, mocking her. She had no indication of where Fiona had gone, only a long-dead daisy kept in a mason jar with an inch of dirty water and a T-shirt she would never wash for fear that the sweet scent of Fiona would fade.

This gift was different, though, because it was in the body of Mayor Nelson Woodfield.

Adeline remembered watching him on local news while sharing a bowl of popcorn with Fiona. After inheriting a prodigious sum of money from some dead relative, Mr. Woodfield had spent a substantial portion of it in a gentlemen's club known as *Bottom's Up* and suffered the effects of the subsequent scandal for which he was giving a feigned apology to the public.

"It's just disgusting," Fiona had said. "Why do they keep electing him?"

"It's only his third term," Adeline said. "Davenport served for six."

"Davenport was sweet. This is Woodfield's third scandal this term."

"Three?"

"There was that thing with his secretary and then the series of emails with that highschooler."

"Right, right," Adeline said, not uninterested but somewhat apathetic on the issue. She shrugged. "People like him. He's charming,"

"He's disgusting." Fiona said, spitting out an unpopped kernel. "How can you work with a pig like that?"

"I don't see him that often. Just for the occasional signature and whatnot."

"I'm bored," Fiona proclaimed, suddenly. "Let's watch *Buffy*."

That was two weeks before Fiona had disappeared.

Three months later, and only a few days before she examined his corpse, Adeline was inspecting the body of an old woman who had been found by a neighbour, her two cats feeding on the carcass, when Mr. Woodfield strode into her operating room.

"Hello, Ms. St. James," he bellowed, forcing Adeline to turn startled, an intestine dangling from her gloved hand.

"Mr. Woodfield," she said, placing her tools down and removing her gloves. "Please, call me Adeline."

"What have we got here?"

"Oh, presumably old age. She was ninety-one."

"Ah, wonderful," Mr. Woodfield said.

Adeline blinked, bewildered.

"So what brings you to visit, Mr. Woodfield?"

"Just checking in with my little doctor."

"I'm not a—"

"Ms. St. James, do you ever find the fear arousing?"

Adeline, puzzled, cocked her head and stared blankly at Mr. Woodfield's shiny forehead, from which she had noticed a sweep of thin grey hair had inched farther away with each mayoral term.

"The blood and guts? Scary isn't it? I find it arousing," he continued.

As Mr. Woodfield moved closer to Adeline, the smell

of a flavoured, rustic cologne infused with the rancid stench of his sweat made Adeline silently gag. She sidestepped to the left.

"I'm sure you've seen the news." Mr. Woodfield advanced. "The thing is, I'm not ashamed. The press think I'd oughta be."

Adeline nodded, taking another step, the back of her knees now against an unoccupied cot.

"I'm a sexual being, Ms. St James."

"Adeline," she croaked.

"I'm a very powerful man, Ms. St James... very powerful."

Following the encounter, Adeline had written Fiona a letter, hoping that she would find it left with a bouquet of flowers at their favourite spot, Ida Irwin's gravestone.

Neither of them knew Ida, but her tombstone inscription, which read "there are always flowers for those who want to see them," seemed apt given Fiona's penchant for leaving gifts that only Adeline could find.

Now, as Adeline examined Fiona's note once again and fingering the familiar writing, she knew that Fiona had certainly found her letter.

She took off her blood-splattered coat and closed her eyes, imagining what Fiona's face might have looked like while plunging the knife into Mr. Woodfield's bulging stomach, a duplicitous smile gracing her lips.

Adeline found herself missing the warmth of Fiona's skin, remembering the soft curve of her face and the sweet smile reserved only for her.

She turned over the paper and noticed, for the first time, writing on the back: "Our spot. 4:00 AM."

The early morning fog sent a damp shiver down Adeline's spine as she wove through the gravestones. It was that liminal

71

time between night and day when the pervading grey transformed the world into inscrutable shapes and sensations.

Adeline spotted Fiona sitting cross-legged and barefoot on Ida Irwin's grave, yellow daisies intertwined into her plaited hair.

"Do me a favour next time," Adeline said, approaching. "Later, please."

"It's beautiful," Fiona said without turning around. "The whole world's asleep."

"Or dead."

As Fiona finally turned and stood, meeting her gaze, Adeline felt herself sink into Fiona's honey eyes. Her familiar floral scent mixed with the fetid smell of decay that permeated the cemetery.

"Kiss me?" Fiona asked, with that tender smile.

Adeline leaned in, pressing her lips against Fiona's, hesitant at first, and then succumbing. Adeline felt a warmth spreading within as she allowed herself to embrace the tantalizing kiss of this intimate vagrant.

"I missed you," Fiona said after pulling away.

"I miss you too," Adeline whispered.

As Fiona took her hand, though, Adeline felt her chest tighten. She remembered the lie she had written so calmly and decidedly on the medical examiner's report. She remembered the sleepless nights alone in bed and the harsh absence of Fiona's touch. She remembered the delicious rapture she had felt with each new gift and the subsequent anxiety and the dejection of knowing Fiona was essentially nothing more than a memory.

"You can't keep doing this," Adeline said, her eyes stinging. "If we can't be together."

Fiona's smile faded.

"It's… it's fine," Fiona stammered. "I'll get a burner phone."

"No, Fiona. It's too much."

"What are you talking about? Addie I—"

"I've been lying on reports," Adeline said. "To protect you."

"So?"

"It's my job."

"Your job matters more than me?" Fiona asked, her eyes watery and wide.

And with force, Adeline answered. "You aren't there." Her voice caught with the last syllable and wavered slightly.

Fiona's innocent face was tormented, blushing red. Her mouth trembled and her eyes, though always iridescent, looked blank and misty.

"I keep trying to forget you so that I can remember what it's like to be alone," Adeline started, her throat contracting as she spoke. "But you keep leaving me reminders."

"You want to forget me?"

Adeline turned, knowing that if she spent a second longer looking at her face, she would bury herself in Fiona's arms and collapse once again into that enticing embrace. She tried to rationalize the ache of desperation and longing and complete despair; it was only a chemical reaction, a dependency she would soon forget on a dream that would always remain unfulfilled.

Then, Adeline sped away into the swirling grey clouds of fog under a line of yew trees at the edge of the cemetery. She dared not look back.

As she fled, some warmth, some passion or fire, drained from her very being. The tips of her fingers tingled and her cheeks burned. Her head brimmed with memories of Fiona, the never-present girl, almost a shadow, whom Adeline wished she could hold. Her stomach twisted with familiar grief as she tried to steady her breath.

73

As her tread slowed and she tried, in vain, not to let her tears fall, a lifeless figure dropped from the branches above, landing only inches from Adeline's feet. It was a squirrel. Adeline knelt, carefully picked up the dead creature, stiff and spiritless, and looked deeply into its cold black eyes. She cocked her head to the left. What had been its final wish?

About the author
Zoe Stanton-Savitz is a recent graduate from Sarah Lawrence College where she studied literature, writing and theatre arts. She writes fiction, non-fiction and plays, and her work has been published in Sarah Lawrence's literary magazines, *The Croaker* and *Love and Squalor*, and in the student newspaper, *The Phoenix*, where Zoe also served as the editor-in-chief for two years. Her work has also been published in *Math Magazine*, *Fresh Words Contemporary One Minute Plays Volume 4* and Wicked Shadow Press *Murder on her Mind Anthology*. Starting in the autumn, Zoe will be attending Columbia University's School of the Arts to begin working towards her MFA in playwriting.

Framed

Linda Flynn

"Life imitates art far more than art imitates Life."
Oscar Wilde

She picked me up like a grubby coin on the pavement. I suppose you could say that I was her lucky penny.

It was on the evening of the funeral. Death came as a relief to my mother. And me. Three decades of disappointment in her only son could not be hidden by homemade meringues and fluffy slippers.

Sometimes a chance for change slips by before you can grab it. I reached out for this one with both arms. She wouldn't give me her name, so I called her Raven.

I should have known from her sleek, silent movements that one day she too would slink into the shadows. Red lips and nails, ambition flowed through her like a warning light.

The bar was in the kind of dark that made you glad you couldn't see the cockroaches. She noticed me; that was enough, as I melted into a dingy pool of pale light and self-pity.

It was hard to count the glasses when they came so slick and easy. It was hard not to talk with her languid arm across my shoulder; it was hard not to look when she draped silkily over me. She made me feel good, so good and her sigh, oh my, I could have blown away on her sigh.

I don't know how we got talking about art. Or my father's gallery. I do know how she listened so well, looking straight at me with those glinting black eyes. Men have fallen for less. My disdainful father once said to me with a sneer, "You're not gifted, you're no art connoisseur. Your knowledge is pitiful!" I might not have had his expertise at recognising paintings, but I had a talent for knowing about people. I told her about my father's contacts, their families, pets, security, holidays, collections.

So the day came when I was clever, useful, valued. There were twelve of us, each doing a different part of the puzzle, without seeing how it all fitted together. My job during the heist was to create diversions around the city, pulling the police in different directions. I triggered store alarms, set fire to parked cars, blocked bridges: a whirling mass of explosions, flames, smoke, sirens. Confusion.

At 21.05 I ran through strobing blue flashes until I reached the brick bridge over the river. In a rowing boat I waited.

I steadied my breath in the dank smell. Water lapped against the sides. Clicking heels approached, tapping in time with the pulsing lights.

Her long arm reached out and I clung to it. Shadows slid along the sharp blades of her cheek bones. Pointing to her lips.

My stomach clenched as I clutched the package. She gave a long, dark stare and told me to meet her in Paris with the painting. Then she slipped away, leaving behind a whisper of her perfume and the glowing red tail light of her cigarette end.

I was born for this. I tore off the wrapping. The gilt frame glowed in my torch light, each ridge narrowing like a tunnel, until my eyes submerged into the blackness of the portrait. And there they stayed.

My father used to say that an instinct for a masterpiece runs through the veins like fiery cognac, your body warming, your senses melting. I had never felt it. Until now.

In that moment I became the winner in a poker game, a king wearing a crown. Someone who mattered.

I didn't see the ripples on the water. I didn't hear the subdued thrum of the motors. Not until I was surrounded. The river police nosed their boats forward, poking mine on all sides.

I should have saved myself. I could have thrown the painting into the river. Instead I clenched it to me as though it pulsed with life. One of the most valuable portraits in the world was in my arms.

Under a bare bulb I stared at a tobacco brown desk. I shook my head at the policeman, "No phone calls. No next of kin." They called in an expert, a friend of my father, to examine the painting. He turned the portrait around, observing it with cold, dead eyes. He examined the back and the placing of the signature. His thin lips curled with disgust as he passed it back and spat, "Fake!"

The detective sighed and looked defeated. "The real painting will be out of the country by now."

Then it clicked: her clever manipulation. My real job hadn't been to activate the decoys, but to become the decoy.

In prison I paint copies of old masters. Every stroke underlines my lack of real talent.

About the author
Linda Flynn has had books published for children and teenagers, which include six with the Heinemann Fiction Project, as well as *Santa's Supersonic Sleigh* which was launched with Chapeltown Publishing in December 2022. *Playing Together* is due out over the next few months. Thirty-three short stories, mainly written for adults, have been published. In addition, she has written for a number of newspapers and magazines, including theatre reviews. Her anthology of short stories, *I Knew it in the Bath* was released in September 2022 with Bridge House. She can be found at: www.lindaflynn.com.

Inheritance

Jemma Marie

I inherited three things from my mother when she died: a charming pair of nineteenth-century diamond earrings that were far too precious to ever take out of the jewellery box, her somewhat senile cocker spaniel, Josephine. And her Kill List.

Not the hypothetical list everybody keeps of the people they'd quite cheerfully throttle given half a chance: that old codger who always parks in your space, Kenny from IT who only makes eye contact with your breasts, the eight-stone-nothing woman in front who orders the iced skinny macchiato with almond milk and an extra shot of salted caramel. But an actual immortal oath of people you have pledged to kill, binding beyond death, to be passed down via your family line until complete.

Yeah, that's exactly what I thought. *What the actual fuck?*

"I can only conclude from your obvious bewilderment that your mother failed to inform you of this bequest prior to her unfortunate demise. Upon completion of the list, whomsoever carries out the final death blow shall receive five million pounds as a token of the State's gratitude."

The ancient-looking Executor of the Wills peered over his spectacles as I struggled to come up with something in the region of a coherent sentence. Eventually, I settled on the most pressing issue.

"But… I can't *kill* people."

"Should the beneficiary refuse to bear responsibility, the oath will automatically transfer to the next member of the bloodline."

As one, our eyes fell upon my two-year-old, Amelia,

who picked up a piece of banana from her highchair tray, and smushed it full force onto her forehead as she let out a piercing array of delighted shrieks.

"This must be some sort of joke," I said, weakly. "My ex-husband's put you up to this hasn't he? That bastard always did have a sick sense of humour."

"I can assure you, Ms. Ferringdon, I am deadly serious." For the first time since his arrival, I saw something steely beneath the sterile surface. What I had mistaken as a tedious lifelessness was something far more akin to *soullessness*. I couldn't detect so much as a flicker of sympathy as he pushed the contract towards me. Despite the utter absurdity of the situation, it was clear that this was indeed happening, and I had absolutely no choice in the matter.

I picked up the pen and committed myself to murder.

The list sat on the dining room table. I circled it warily, unwilling to flip it over and look my fate in the face. Futile as it may seem, I wished to remain the person I was now for as long as possible, already knowing my life would now be formed of *before* and *after*.

My relationship with my mother had always been, shall we say, fraught. She was cold and controlling, quick to judge and impossible to please, but the idea of her as a killer was inconceivable. And the notion that I was about to take up the mantle, even more so.

How was I supposed to go about it for starters? As a 5 ft 4, born and bred city girl, I was hardly a dab hand with a weapon, nor was I likely to win any fights based on brute strength. And what if I got caught? What would happen to me, to Amelia?

The impossibility of my situation engulfed me, hatred towards my mother clawing its way from the inside out until I could bear it no longer. I threw the jewellery box against the wall, screaming my frustration as it shattered, and sank to the floor in breathless sobs. One of the earrings rolled slowly across the floorboards towards me, its diamond cracked almost in half. As I picked it up, it split open and a tiny, liquid-filled vial dropped into my lap.

My God, the mad old bat had gone and left me her poison.

With the method of murder now decided and a bracing swig of Jack Daniel's, I summoned what little courage I had and flipped over the tiny piece of paper. The list contained over fifty names but almost all of them had been struck through, leaving only two untouched.

My eyes caught on the last name, and I felt the world shift once more beneath my feet.

Christopher Henry Ferringdon

Of all the names I could have found, my brother's was the very last I had expected to see.

Emotionally absent, my mother left my big brother, Christopher to raise me after my father quietly disappeared one Sunday evening, without a backwards glance. Kit was my rock; big brother, surrogate dad and best friend all rolled into one, the only source of light and love in my otherwise broken childhood, and the one person I relied on most in the world.

Cradling the whiskey bottle, I drank myself into the blissful stupor of oblivion.

"Wakey up, Mummyyy!" Groaning, I scraped my tongue off the roof of my mouth and opened one bleary eye.

Amelia's face loomed inches from my own, her head tipped sideways to examine this interesting new development that was her drunken mother.

Heaving myself upright, I attempted to switch on

normality enough to get us functioning and ready for nursery, so I could plot the impossible, uninterrupted. Fifty-three minutes, two tantrums and one drop-off later, I sat on the sofa gazing sightlessly at the TV as I tried to steer my booze-addled brain into some form of acceptance and planning.

"The body of twenty-three-year-old Amanda Linton has been formally identified after she was involved in a hit-and-run late last night."

I froze as the name registered. Snatching up the remote, I stabbed at the volume button, but the reporter was already moving onto the next headline. Hands trembling, I seized the list from where I'd dropped it last night and searched the small collection of unmarked names at the bottom. It wasn't there. My eyes scanned the list again and with a jolt, I saw what I had missed the first time – my brother's name remained untouched, but just above it sat:

Amanda Elizabeth Linton.

My mind scrambled hopelessly for something resembling a rational explanation, other than the terrifying notion that this list contained some kind of horrific sentient essence. I put my head in my hands and focused on not losing my shit completely. But in the darkness, all I could see were Kit's laughing brown eyes and easy smile. Of all the people on this Earth, he was the one I simply could not kill.

But perhaps I wouldn't have to. Not right now at least. With only one name left to complete the list, I could wait for years, decades even, until we were old and grey and had lived our lives. I hadn't been responsible for Amanda's death, and yet the list counted her as taken care of, so Kit would surely be the same.

I started to pace as I tried to play out all the ramifications of waiting. It was a risk – if I died first, I knew Amelia would then be responsible for having to kill her uncle. But at nine

81

years his junior, the probability of me outliving him was high, so the risk was calculated; as long as the commitment to kill was there, the timing could be manipulated. Laughing, I felt the giddiness of relief wash over me. It was all going to be okay.

That night I lay in bed, floating just on the border of sleep, when an image drifted into my mind of the ominous old man who had delivered this nightmare to my doorstep, and I suddenly remembered there had been a second piece of paper.

Unease forced me upright and, stumbling to the kitchen, I scanned the messy countertops until my eyes landed on what had yesterday been a crisp white sheet, but was now sticky with small, jammy fingerprints. Skipping impatiently past the rules relating to the oath being passed down via bloodline and the five million pounds recompense, my eyes alighted on a section mid-way down.

Orders of the Oath

You must pledge to kill no fewer than twenty souls. A maximum of three additional names may be added to the list at your discretion. On each anniversary of the list's inception, should it remain incomplete, one additional name shall be added.

I felt the consequences of that final line hit me full force – the years I had banked on snatched away in an instant, leaving a ticking timebomb in its wake. I had no idea how names were determined. What if the next one was my niece? Or my nephew? And even if I took the risk, how many people could I kill to save my brother?

I scanned the words again, hoping for a hidden loophole. *On each anniversary of the list's inception...*

Dread settled in the pit of my stomach, as I scrambled back up the stairs to where I'd left the list. Snatching it up from my bedside table, a low moan escaped me as I registered the date.

Tuesday 21st April 1981

Oh God, I had three days.

The next forty-eight hours passed in a dream-like haze. I washed, I ate, I dressed, I kissed and cuddled and played with Amelia, but inside, a war raged. I plotted my brother's murder whilst all the time dismissing the reality that I would truly go through with it. Until suddenly it was day three and I was out of time.

"Luce! This is a surprise. Everything alright?" Kit's usually care-free face creased into a slight frown at finding me on his doorstep.

"Yes, yes. Everything's fine! Just fancied a catch up with my big bro." I could feel my cheeks pulling too tight as I dragged the smile across my face.

Kit eyed me for a few moments before his face relaxed into a wide grin and he threw open the door.

"Fancy a cuppa?"

Following him to the kitchen, I tried to concentrate over the hammering of my heart, as he prattled cheerfully on about his latest sale at work.

"Is Lydia here?" I asked, as he paused to glance over at my uncharacteristic silence.

"No, she's with the kids. She volunteered as a helper for their school trip at the local museum. They'll be bored senseless, the poor sods." He chuckled to himself, shaking his head.

A deep ache grew within me as I watched him pottering around the kitchen, the everyday act of tea-making made notable by the cold knowledge of imminent loss. I couldn't do this.

"Kit…"

DING-DONG!

"Finish those off, will you?" He called over his shoulder. "It'll be another of Lydia's packages. That woman never stops shopping."

The spell broken, I gathered the tatters of my resolve and strode over to the two steaming mugs. This was my chance. I quickly added in the sugar, then slipped the vial of poison from my pocket and quickly poured the contents into the left-hand mug.

"What are you up to, sis?"

I jumped guiltily, almost sending both drinks crashing to the ground.

"What do you mean?" I asked, trying desperately to keep the fear from my voice.

"Well, not that I'm not chuffed to see you, but you don't usually just drop by…"

My whole body sagged in relief.

"Oh. Um, I wanted to borrow one of your brochures. I'm thinking of getting a new print to hang above the sofa and thought, why not one of my big brother's pieces?"

I hadn't imagined it was possible to feel any worse, but as Kit's eyes lit up, I felt another wave of guilt engulf me. Holding back the looming grief, I watched him unknowingly pick up his death sentence and followed him to the study.

"Here, let me show you this new collection we've got coming out." Grabbing both cups, he placed them on the windowsill and shooed me over to the ottoman where his brochures lay splayed in a picture-perfect display. Leafing through the pages, I tried to block out the images of Kit as young boy, painting in the garden as I watched in awed delight. Tears pricked my eyes and I quickly dashed them away as I heard my brother rustling through the shelves behind me.

"This one might be just what you're after, Luce."

Turning, I picked up my mug and took a big gulp to buy another moment to compose myself.

"Oh wow, these are beautiful," I said, turning the pages of the catalogue.

"You take your time. I'm just going to nip to the loo a sec."

Hearing his footsteps retreat down the hallway, I allowed the façade to drop and felt the sheer weight of my misery crushing me. Laying down the brochures, I drifted over to the desk, letting my fingers trace the smiling portraits. The corner of a page caught my eye and I pulled it from beneath the book it rested under.

The Kill List of Madeline Eliza Ferringdon

And at the very bottom of the list sat one name.

Lucy Sylvia Ferringdon

My vision swam as I stared in disbelief at the list in front of me. Heart thudding in my ears, I struggled to comprehend how this could have happened. I clutched the desk to stay upright, as a sudden wave of dizziness washed over me.

"I'm so sorry, Luce," came a quiet voice from behind me.

I stumbled as I tried to turn, the mug dropping from my hands and smashing on the floorboards below. My legs gave way beneath me as I realised what Kit had done.

There was so much I needed to say.

I wanted to scream and curse him for what he had done.

To beg his forgiveness for what I had attempted to do.

Tell him I hated him for leaving Amelia without a mother.

Tell him I loved him for being my big brother.

But the words caught in my throat as it began to close up, and all I could do was watch Kit walk over to me as I lay convulsing on his floor in helpless horror.

He laid a gentle hand on my cheek, as the tears flowed unchecked down both our faces, and the world slowly faded into darkness.

About the author
Jemma Marie is a Bristol-born writer, happily settled in Cardiff. She likes quintessential writerly things, such as cats and curling up with a good book, and has been working on her first novel for the past few years. She'll be making it to Chapter 3 any day now...

Just a Packet of Seeds

Paula R C Readman

"Stop, Ella! What are you trying to do, get us dismissed?" Ella dropped the pile of dirty towels. "Oh, I'm sorry." Ella shook her head, knowing it would've been an expensive mistake, if the coloured towels had gone down the chute marked whites only. The laundrette would've ground to a halt, too, while the error was sorted out.

"Please snap out of it, and keep your mind on your job," Julie said passing another load of whites to her before bending to retrieve the offending articles. "The hotels won't be happy, if all their whites went back pink."

The two women carried on in silence, sorting through the piles of laundry that arrived by the lorry load.

"I'm sorry. I can't shake myself out of the blues." Ella sighed and pushed her dark brown hair back from her sweaty forehead before tossing another pile of towels into the right chute. The washing disappeared, with a whoosh, and slid down into the large industrial washers. "I shouldn't be working here, sorting out other people's dirty washing, but outside getting my hands dirty doing what I've been trained to do, and love best of all – landscape gardening."

Julie smiled. "I know, love. You're just too qualified to be here. It's such a shame you couldn't get the job, you wanted when you left uni. No time like the present, as they say, so you know what you've got to do?"

"I know, but what do I say?"

"Tell your husband how you're feeling. I'm sure he'll understand."

"Oh, Julie, he's just so shattered when he comes in from work. I don't like to bother him."

"But, it bothers you working here; you should be

87

following your heart and have a house with a garden. Why don't you give the estate agent a ring, find out more. It can't do any harm, especially when your husband is so busy. After all, it's the sort of place you both want. I reckon a guardian angel must have been watching when the estate agent messed up, and sent you those details by mistake."

On her way home, Ella paused at the estate agent's door, and took a deep breath before entering. Moments later, she was heading home. When they first moved into the flat five years ago it was great, but now, most of their friends had moved into houses, in readiness to start a family. Ella was pleased for them, but starting a family was the last thing on her mind as her plan was to start her landscaping business. Dan had concerns about saddling themselves with a huge loan to buy a house.

"I want us to buy our *forever* home, not just one to keep up with our friends."

Ella had agreed with her husband. Most of their friends had bought town houses with easy access to the centre of London. "We need to be where the action is and close to the city nightlife," they had said.

Their friends weren't interested in growing things, apart from a family. Ella longed for a home surrounded by green spaces, but none of the houses they had seen so far offered her what she wanted, and within their price range. Ella tried to quell the growing disappointment in her stomach as she ran up the stairs to their second-floor flat, in a converted office block, and slipped the key into the door.

From their small kitchen area, she glanced out the French windows to a collection of odd-sized pots and containers that stood on the balcony. Having the balcony was one of the reasons they had stretched their limited budget to buy the spacious flat, with its two bedrooms and open-planned living room. Ella sighed, once she'd been happy here. On warm summer evenings, over a wonderful meal Ella had prepared, they'd share a glass or two amidst the pots of geraniums and the summer jasmine in their rooftop haven. In the early days, there had been time to share a leisurely breakfast together before they both headed off to work, but now those dreamy, shared moments were long gone as Dan rushed to catch his train.

Ella sat with her cup of tea and toasted cheese sandwich, watching the sun setting, knowing Dan was working late again. She hated eating alone, though this evening her heart felt even heavier. The estate agent had told her that someone had made a reserved offer on the house. Why hadn't she spoken to Dan earlier instead of allowing her indecision to get in the way? She could have put in an offer, and then told him about it afterwards.

Maybe they were still in with a chance, if they moved quickly. The agent had explained that the prospective buyers might withdraw their offer at the last minute. As it was Saturday tomorrow, she might be able to persuade Dan to take the day off to look at the house. If they both liked it, then maybe, he would agree to put in a higher bid. Happy with the thought that she was doing something positive at last, Ella washed up her tea things, showered, and got ready for bed.

Refreshed by the shower, Ella sat in her pyjamas, with the designs for her dream garden spread out on the bed before her. Ever since the estate agent details had arrived at the flat, she had been working on them. As she moved one of the gardening books aside, she sighed deeply on catching sight of the page marker. The property details had arrived quite unexpectedly through the post a few weeks ago. On it, a photograph showed a neglected Victorian house, standing in a large, untidy garden. The caption read "*in much need of love and attention*". The moment Ella read those words, she wanted the house, well, not so much the house, but more the once well-loved garden. In the photo, she could just make out some well-established trees and shrubs.

From somewhere far off, on a light, summer breeze, a soft voice called Ella's name, as she walked through a garden surrounded by all her favourite flowers. From the tall hollyhocks of soft yellows and oranges to the blues of delphiniums, the bright yellow face of sunflowers to the dark greens of the shrubs and the lawn, covered in white daisies, while overhead a tall, single silver birch moved in time with the breeze.

"Come on, Ella, wake up. It's time to get into bed properly."

Opening her eyes, she found Dan studying her drawings. "These are good," he said.

Ella moved the book, with the property details aside, and sat up. "They're nothing much really, just idle sketches."

"I like this logo, it's great." Dan held up a stylised picture of a silver birch.

"It's for my landscaping business, someday, maybe," she said sleepily.

Dan slid his arm round her shoulder. "Ella, I know how much it would mean to you, if we were able to move, but…"

Ella silenced him with a kiss, while pushing the book, containing the agent's details, out of sight. She knew what his "*but*" meant. He was working too many hours as it was, making her need for a garden seem all the more selfish, but if she had one to occupy her, she wouldn't feel so lonely, and could start building her business. Dan had promised that this year, they would start looking for their forever home, but so far, he'd been either too busy, or too tired to even look online.

On waking, Ella turned to find Dan was gone. She checked her phone, and was puzzled to find the alarm hadn't gone off yet. Why hadn't he woken her, to say good-bye?

The bedroom door swung open and Dan stood holding a tray. "Good morning, sweetheart. I thought we would have breakfast in bed." He set the tray before her.

"But, haven't you got work, today?"

"Nope! I wanted to make time for us," he said passing her a mug of coffee before placing his mug on the bedside cabinet. "You know what they say about Jack being a dull boy." Dan's grey eyes sparkled with excitement as he bent to kiss her.

"But, what about that order you've been working on?"

"We completed it yesterday, that's why I was late in. And, the company have renewed their order, meaning our employees' jobs are safe because it's improved our viability too." Dan pulled Ella close. "So instead of dashing for a train this morning, I get to cuddle you in bed."

"That's such wonderful news, Dan."

"About the jobs... or me cuddling you?" He laughed.

"Both," Ella replied with a giggle.

After Ella finished eating her toast and marmalade, Dan slipped his arm around her shoulder and pulled her into him. "What are your plans for this weekend?"

"I don't really have one but..." Ella slipped from his arms, and reached for the house details. "Well, I was planning on taking a look at this," she said. "I know, we..." Ella handed him her bookmarker.

"Hey, what's this?" Dan unfolded it.

"A house with a big garden," she said.

"But…"

Ella cut him off, "I know we can't afford it, but can we just take a look, please."

"It says here, in need of love and attention. That sounds expensive."

"We're only looking." Ella gave a nervous smile.

"Hmm, it sounds very interesting." Dan took a sip of his coffee. "Did you want to go today?"

"Could we… it looks bright out." Ella leapt from the bed, nearly knocking the coffee from Dan's hand. How many times had she dreamt about wandering through the neglected garden, and today she would get to see what wonders lay hidden within it.

"You make us a fresh drink. I'll give the estate agency a ring."

"Thank you. I promise not to fall in love with it, but it would be nice to take a look." Ella inhaled sharply, trying to control her excitement.

Dan smiled and shook his head gently, his eyes sparkling with laughter. "I don't believe that for one minute. Maybe, not the house, but you'll fall in love with the garden." He held up the badly creased details. "May I ask how long you've had these?"

"A couple of weeks… I wanted to tell you sooner, but you had enough to worry about with the order at work. I found out, yesterday someone has put in a bid, but we can still take a look, can't we?"

"Have they? Are you sure you still want to go, Ella?"

"Please."

"Okay. Let's forget about the drinks. You start getting ready and I'll give them a ring."

Ella took the tray into the kitchen, and set to work washing up the breakfast things. As she was drying, Dan's favourite mug, it slipped from her hand. "Oh no!" She grabbed for it before it hit the floor. Taking a deep breath, Ella held the cup to her as a wave of apprehension mixed with excitement bubbled in her. Putting the cup back in the cupboard, she dashed to the bedroom to get dressrd just as Dan came out the bathroom.

Leaving the city behind, the route Dan took led them down a series of twisting country lanes, filled with hedgerows of white and pink blossoms, while yellows and violet-coloured flowers carpeted the ground. Ella noticed too that Dan seemed more relaxed than he had been in a long time.
 Was this their new beginning? She hoped so.
 The satnav soon let them know they had arrived at their destination. The house stood on its own plot, surrounded on three sides by a high hedge and beyond farmland. On hearing Dan exhale deeply, Ella wanted to cry. She daren't turn to look at her husband in fear of seeing his reaction to the state of the house. The photographs hadn't shown the full extent of the repairs needed to make it habitable. Dan would be calculating the cost of repairing the roof, and as for the chimney, it looked to be on the lean. The front of the house displayed impressive graffiti-covered boards over the downstairs windows. Just as Ella plucked up the courage to ask Dan what he was thinking, the estate agent arrived. As they went to meet the agent, he proffered his hand.
 "Mr and Mrs Harding? I'm James Brouwer. Lovely morning for it. A marvellous opportunity for anyone with the ability to think outside the box. Many of its original features are still in situ, too," the estate agent said without taking a breath. As James unlocked the door, Ella tried to catch her husband's eye, but he was too busy studying the peeling paint. After pushing the door open, James said, "I must warn you both to take care inside."

James guided them through to the kitchen, pointing out the butler sink and cooking range. Ella glanced at Dan as he took in the broken glass, boarded-up windows and moth-eaten carpets. Not only did the house reek of damp, it was visible in the peeling paper and paint. Upstairs, they gingerly avoided areas of the floorboards where the ceiling had come down after the rain had seeped through the roof. In the back bedroom, James said, "Look at the lovely vista. The French window leads onto a balcony."

As Dan followed the estate agent onto the landing, Ella glimpsed out the French window and looked down onto a tangle of weeds and shrubs. "Oh, you're so much more than my dream," she whispered to the house.

A crazy pavement twisted its way through an overgrown lawn to a gate in a high hedge, and beyond it, the only thing Ella could see was the top of a dancing silver birch that shimmered pale green in the bright sunshine. "There has to be a secret garden, beyond the hedge," Ella said softly. "Oh, to have chance to tame the wild tangle of brambles, stinging nettles, and thistles, with hollyhocks, sunflowers and delphiniums."

"Ella, come on…" Dan called from downstairs.

Outside, Dan was chatting with James as Ella joined them. After the estate agent had locked up, and waved them goodbye, they walked over to their car. From the car, Ella studied the house. It had everything she wanted. The rooms would be light and spacious, and both she and Dan could have an office space of their own. Ella turned to tell her husband, what she thought of the house, but the look on his face made her heart sink. It hadn't made a good impression on him, she was sure.

"It needs a lot of work, doesn't it?" Dan finally spoke his thoughts.

94

"Yes, it does."

"It's a bit off the beaten track too, don't you think?" Dan gave the house another cursory glance before pulling off the weed-covered drive. Ella nodded, unable to speak as the house and garden grew smaller in the car wing mirror before disappearing from view. As the satnav guided them through the winding lanes, Dan spoke.

"Do you really think you could put up with living out here, Ella, with no shops just around the corner?"

"Maybe…" Ella lowered her head, trying not to show her disappointment, after all, he'd warned her. It wasn't fair to spoil their first weekend they had together in months.

Back at the flat, while Dan disappeared to sort out some company paperwork, Ella prepared lunch. As she buttered the rolls, she wondered whether it was worth suggesting looking at what else was on offer via the net.

"Dan, I was wondering…" Ella began as they finished their desserts.

Dan looked up, but then his phone rang. "Hello, yes."

Ella hoped it wasn't his business partner. She watched as her husband's face changed from serious to a gentle smile, and then he winked at her.

"Yes. I understand, no harm done. I'm sorry I just couldn't get to see it sooner. Of course, she is. Great doing business with you, thank you." Dan switched off his phone.

"They don't want you back in work today, do they?" Ella picked up her wine glass and took a sip.

"No, it wasn't about work. Anyway, we should spend more time together. So what did you think of the property? You were very quiet on the way home."

"The property?" What could she say? Dan didn't like it.

"Please don't tell me you've changed your mind."

She shook her head; the words wouldn't come.

"Oh, Ella... I've just transferred the deposit over." Dan took a deep breath. "I knew I should've spoken to you about it, but it was meant to be a surprise. The details should've come to me at work. We were the other prospective buyers, I'd put in a holding bid until this weekend, knowing the order would be finished. When I saw the drawings of the garden, I thought you would be happy there."

Ella swallowed, trying to stop the sudden rush of tears. She went to wipe them away, but Dan swept her into his arms and kissed her wet cheeks.

"Hey, my love, don't cry, I'm supposed to make you happy."

"Oh, Dan, is it really ours?" Her words came at last.

"Yes! You're pleased, aren't you?"

"More than I can say, but I didn't think you liked it. The costs to do the repairs will be a fortune."

"I've already called in some favours, from some of my university friends who are in the building trade. With the overtime, I've done, and the future overtime, you'll have nothing to worry about, but your new garden. Oh, and I've got a little something for you to start it off." He reached into his pocket. "Sorry, it isn't much, just a packet of seeds."

"Oh, but Dan, from little seeds, a wonderful garden will grow," Ella said before kissing him.

About the author
Paula R C Readman is married and lives in Essex, England. In 2020 her first crime novella, *The Funeral Birds*, was published by Demain Publishing, and a single collection of short stories, *Days Pass Like A Shadow* was published by Bridge House Publishing. Darkstroke Books published her first crime novel, *Stone Angels*, and since then they have published *Seeking the Dark* and *The Phoenix Hours*. Paula is now working on her seventh book.

Lost in Translation

Maria Kinnersley

"Is it ready yet?"

Candy looked over at the young apprentice and frowned as she caught sight of the bored expression on her little face. *She was going to have to show more interest if Candy was going to keep her on.*

"All good things take time, Alphina," she replied. "Another couple of hours will do it. Then it needs to cool before any further work can be done."

This news was greeted with a heavy sigh and muttering, which she chose to ignore.

She continued her careful stirring. If the girl did but know it, they had reached a strategic point in the process. Candy always enjoyed this part and likened it to baking a cake. She knew that it was only if everything were done correctly that she could create what her client had asked for.

The object being made today was a cat that had been so precious to its owner. It had died recently, and the client wanted a duplicate. She had travelled far and was prepared to pay any price for the restoration of her beloved pet; not that money was of importance to this user of magic.

Candy was a young witch with a gift. She could transform things that had recently died and translate the materials to make replacements. Although a senior witch had trained her, as she was now training Alphina, it had been obvious to her teacher that Candy was an instinctive maker who had accomplished things far beyond her own skills.

She reached up and pushed back a stray curly copper tress which refused to stay within the loose ponytail tied when she commenced this work. As she moved to retrieve a ladle, the random golden markings in her soft shift dress travelled with her moving like butterflies around her.

She was loved and respected in the village of Venta and lived in a small round cottage on the edge of the village, next to a river that ran outside her home. It was the reason that she chose to live here. Water was particularly useful for her work.

Like all of her kind, she used her skills for the good of the people that lived nearby. Pills and potions were her stock in trade, making her the "medicine woman" of the village.

She thought back to when she had first come there. She'd learnt all she could from her teacher, who was also her mother. As tradition demanded, she had left home to seek a village that would welcome her.

When she arrived at Venta, a small isolated windswept village, she was initially treated with distrust. They had never had one of her kind there. She kept to herself, picked the location of her home. Then, overnight, she constructed the little round, thatched dwelling so unlike any other in that small settlement.

When the villagers experienced the benefits of having her in their community, with people being healed and practical problems solved, she became accepted within the village. Word spread of her skills, with numerous needy souls coming from great distances for her help.

Next to her home was her workroom, so unlike the shed that many assumed it was. From the outside, it looked tiny, a place used for storage. Anyone who entered, as Alphina had done on her first day, was astounded by the space inside.

Candy's cauldron was in the centre of the room, vital for much of her special work. Given to her by her mother, it contained mysteries. Even Candy was still learning those wonderful things that could be created from the depths of this vessel.

The use of her extraordinary gift wasn't something she exercised often. Her healing skills alone made her renowned. But this other talent was something that was passed through word of mouth, to those in need of it.

"Don't be too free with your talent," Freeda, her mother said, before she left home. "People won't respect it for the precious thing that it is. You don't want to see what you have given abused."

So, Candy would spend much time with the petitioner wanting the restoration of a treasured object or, more rarely, a pet. Only when she was certain there was worth in their request did she consider it. Not everyone gained what they wanted. Money was not part of it. Witches in the main were not governed by gold or coins, only by the common good they could bring to others. True, there were witches who toyed with humans and brought them pain, but they were not in the majority.

Bringing herself back from her thoughts, Candy leaned forward, and looked into the cauldron, then sniffed.

"It's ready," she said, the tone in her voice indicating a pronouncement of a major event.

"About time," murmured Alphina, as she left her position by the wall and came closer.

Candy shot her a look, but the girl returned a neutral gaze.

"You know, Alphina," she said, her tone casual. "You don't have to be my apprentice. No one asked you. No one put you forward. You begged me, remember?"

There was a silence as her apprentice looked down, as she appeared to consider her next words. Candy noticed there a slight shake to the young girl's hands.

"Forgive me, teacher," she said, her voice low. "This

teaching is hard. I hadn't realised there was so much waiting and watching." She paused. "I thought I would get to do spells, easy ones, that it would be exciting."

Candy gave a short snort, followed by a laugh. "Alphi, dear. You are nowhere near ready for spells. True, you have the light within in you to create. I know that. But you must be ready to learn and to observe."

Alphina smiled back, relieved she hadn't annoyed the teacher witch. She knew Candy was usually even-tempered, but when she did get annoyed, things happened, and you didn't want to be in the centre of it.

"Come closer. See what has to happen now. Oh, and bring the box."

Alphina walked over and used the small trolley placed there to move what looked like a wooden box with a lid. It was beautifully carved. With its lid open it appeared empty.

Candy put her hands into the gloopy mixture in the cauldron and reached around.

"Got it," she said happily as her hands left the mixture in the cauldron with a bundle of... Alphina gazed at the amorphous mass.

"What is it?" she asked.

"Something that will be translated," the witch answered, with a secret smile. "And don't ask me how. It's magic!" She manoeuvred the object into the box. "Give me a hand with this, Alphi. It needs to go into the cupboard."

As she helped place the box, she was aware of a faint smell, which quickly disappeared, just leaving her with the mystery of it all.

Twenty-four hours later, they returned to the workroom. Candy opened the box to find not one cat but several. She laughed.

"I shall have to work out why that keeps happening," as she viewed the felines, all with the same markings." She turned to her apprentice. "You see, I'm still learning. You're not the only one."

"Thank you so much," Geena, a middle-aged woman dressed in sumptuous clothing enthused. "I thought I would never see my cat again. And you have given me so much more," she continued, wide-eyed.

She gazed in wonder at the collection of animals in the wicker basket.

"Consider it a bonus. You have paid me well," Candy said with a short bow. She turned to go back into her cottage.

"One thing," said the woman.

The witch turned back, her look questioning. Geena stood there for a moment, temporarily speechless. Twice she opened her mouth, as if to say something, then closed it. The third time she seemed to pluck up courage for this request.

"I have… a friend," she said hesitantly. "He was extremely interested in what you were capable of. He asked me to ask for your help for something he no longer has and desperately wants."

"I need to see him before I can make a decision," said the witch crisply, her faded brown eyes looking intently at the woman, who almost squirmed under her gaze. "Tell him to come to see me. I will decide then."

"That's the problem. He cannot come to you. He is aware of your need for secrecy, but he is an important person who also requires secrecy. He requests your presence."

Candy narrowed her eyes and frowned. After a moment, she gave a nod.

Geena gave a relieved sigh. "Good. I'll send him a message."

"I'd like you to bring back my wife."

Candy's eyes widened as she drew a sharp breath. She

101

was still getting over the shock that the person she had agreed to meet was the Crown Prince of the country. Now his request gave her another surprise.

"Your Highness," she began, "this is something I have never done before."

"But you have brought things back to life?" he said, interrupting her.

"Not brought back to life exactly. I have used the material I have been given to translate it, to make replicas, if you like." She paused, her eyes gazing into the distance. "This would be the largest... project I have ever attempted." She looked at him. Her face wore a slight frown. "And what would people say if she suddenly appeared?"

"They don't know she's dead," he said tersely. "All believe she is away visiting her parents." He looked down at her slight form with a smile. "Will you do it?"

She sighed. "What do you have of hers?"

"Just this," he said producing a hairbrush.

"Her hairs only, I hope."

"It was her individual property. No one else would dare use it."

From a pocket in her tunic, she brought out a bag and opening it, she brought it close to him and he dropped the brush into it.

"I will try," she whispered, as she bowed low.

She did nothing for the first few days. While she set Alphina menial jobs around the workroom, she sat gazing at the bag her face set in deep concentration. Now and again, the young girl glanced at her teacher, who showed no movement or awareness of her presence.

At the end of the second day, Candy stretched and stood up from the stool in front of the bag. Alphina placed herself next to her.

"Do you need anything, teacher?"

Candy looked down at her. Her apprentice was struck by her calm demeanour.

"Alphi, we have work to do. I shall need your help."

Both worked hard, cleaning the workroom and preparing the area for the work that Alphina still didn't know about. She had asked, of course, but the witch had just smiled.

"You will see."

The last job was cleaning the cauldron; work that was Candy's province. She produced an ancient book, the pages browned, but the curly print still black and legible. Words were muttered and many passes were made with her hands over the mouth of the vessel. Alphina looked on wide-eyed, understanding none of it. The words that she could hear made no sense and were hardly audible.

Finally, Candy pronounced, "All is ready. We begin tomorrow."

Alphina was thrilled with the word *"we"*. At last, she was involved.

The following day saw them standing around the cauldron in the centre of the room. To one side was a box similar in style to the one used for the cat, only much bigger. Alphina glanced at Candy. She appeared back to her old self, brisk and business-like. She started as the witch turned to her.

"Hold out your hands."

Alphina lifted her hands, palms up. Carefully the witch slipped a brush from the bag that she placed it, the bristles facing upwards.

"Now I want you, Alphi, very carefully," she stressed with each word, "to use those tweezers on the table to pull hairs from this brush. Each one is to be dropped into the cauldron. Get as many of them as you can. Don't contaminate anything."

Alphina's hand shook as she reached for the tweezers.

She had never been so involved before. Slowly, then with increasing speed she pulled out each hair, then released it, letting each fall into the vessel.

Meanwhile, Candy was occupied bringing the other ingredients together. She glanced over to check on her apprentice.

"Stop," she shouted.

Alphina froze.

"Even I can see that the hairs you are putting in aren't the same, you silly girl," hissed Candy. "Let me look."

Mutely, the young girl held up the brush which the witch examined closely.

"There are only two hairs left that would be hers, do you see?" she said, pointing with her elegant fingers.

Alphina nodded.

"Then pull those out and drop them in my cauldron. Let's hope you've done no harm."

Two days later, two sleep-deprived figures stumbled from the workroom pushing the trolley on which rested the large box.

"I want this close by," Candy explained. "What I have done is new to me and I shall have to keep an eye on it."

So, while Alphina gratefully sought the comfort of her bed, her teacher settled in her favourite armchair to keep a watchful eye on her new creation. But her activities had tired her, and she was soon asleep.

Candy woke with a jump to see someone standing over her. Looking to the side, she saw the box was open. She returned her gaze to the figure, who was still there, her head on one side like... a cat. She studied the eyes. They were bigger than that of a human. It didn't make her look ugly. She looked extraordinary. And beautiful.

She sent a message to the Crown Prince to inform him that his "package" was ready. A little note was included.

I'm sorry but there appears to have been contamination within the brush. Your wife, I believe looks different from how you remembered her. No payment is required if you are not satisfied.

A carriage soon arrived and the woman that had been created for the Crown Prince left in it. Candy was thoughtful as the conveyance disappeared from view.

Time passed. Candy busied herself producing and renewing her stock of potions, taking care to teach Alphina the simpler tasks. They were disturbed during one of their batch cooking exercises by a knock on the door.

She opened the door and found a man waiting outside. With a flourish, he handed over a casket, bowed, and returned to the carriage. They both stood and stared at the vehicle as it disappeared from view.

The witch brought the casket inside and opened it. It was filled to the brim with gold. On top was a letter, which she opened.

Thank you for the work you have done. My wife is perfect, better than before. You see, I killed her because she was having an affair, something I later regretted. What you have translated from her hair is far better. I now have an affectionate and loving wife. I am grateful to you for her.

About the author
Maria started writing a few years ago following early retirement due to ill health. Her first writing efforts were editions of the parish magazine of her church. She has published a few non-fiction articles and has had a short story previously published in an anthology. At present, she's working on a collection of short stories with a couple of draft novels waiting to be edited. She lives in Devon.

Magic Happen'

Gail Schoepple

No Baby

There was once a girl with the particular ability to make magic happen.

"Millie the witch. Millie the witch," her schoolmates would whisper.

Am I a witch? Millie asked.

No baby, a vessel. You're a vessel. It replied.

She kept her eyes down, hands holding her books nice and tight in case someone slapped them out of her grip. Her teeth grinded and clenched – oh boy did she want to make magic happen to these kids.

But she couldn't. Ma spanked her ass hard when that magic started happening and Pa's fingers itched to grab the gun. So she swallowed the magic down and kept it there in her gut, making herself pregnant with it. Can't let the school people *see* it, only let them *know* it.

Ma told the Pastor when it first started and Pastor told his wife and wife told friend and friend told other friend and other friend's son overheard and son goes to school so now school knows that Millie can make magic happen.

William, the boy who sat beside her in the school house, pulled on her braid and hissed, "Demon," but when she turned to glower at him, he was writing in his school book, acting like he did nothn'. She kept quiet and sunk deeper into her chair.

Gotta Go

"Jesus, Laura, are we really just going? Just like that?" Millie's Pa watched Millie's Ma pace through the small square of their home. "They might burn her, Laura. You want her to burn?"

106

"It don't matter what the townsfolk do with it." Millie's Ma froze and seized her torso with a wince on her face. "Frank, I can't stand living beside that curse, I just can't. When it's near… my womb, my womb can feel the darkness left behind. Frank, that child cursed us. We gotta go."

Millie's Pa frowned at Millie's Ma but after a moment he let out a chimney sigh, and nodded, "Alright, Laura. Let's get our things."

Lord Have Mercy

Millie walked home alone, keeping her lunch pail still at her side with her books dunked beside the apple she didn't eat that day. Sun was bright, leaves were changing, grass was high; Millie made it safely behind the gate of her front yard and she scurried behind the front door.

She dropped her pail, startled, and took a step back, bumping against the door.

"Millie Yerlov." Pastor dried his tears with his sleeve.

"Yessir," she replied, still and straight as a beagle's tail.

"Lord have mercy, Millie Yerlov. I don't got the words to tell you this," he said.

Millie waited for him to continue, but he wasn't lying, he really didn't got the words. So Millie said, "Speak." and he spoke.

"Your Ma and Pa's gone."

"They dead?" she asked.

"No child. They ran off."

Hmm, quite an interesting turn of events, it said.

"Who's gonna keep me?" she asked.

"Well, I believe the church will." He shuddered and Millie realized why he was crying. It wasn't because Ma and Pa left, it was because they left him with *her.*

"I see. I'll go pack my things."

She's Gonna Make That Magic Happen

"Stay still, witch." One of the church women held Millie against her chest. She whispered prayers as Pastor approached in a white garment and a gold bowl in his hands. His fingers dipped into the bowl and sneezed the contents all over her face. She squirmed. The whispered prayers grew louder and the people sitting in the pews outstretched their arms. She saw William sitting next to his dad. Smirking.

"May the demon be exuded from this child's body!" Pastor raged, spraying more holy water at her.

She quickly concluded that this public humiliation would not end unless she was exorcized so Millie screamed, and shook her body. The woman released her and stepped back and Pastor hesitated, fingers marinating in holiness. For a moment, the entire church went quiet. Millie decided to fall and as her body landed, the sun started to peek through the stained glass, colours covering her like a quilt.

The church erupted in praise, feet stomping, voices praising God, hands clapping. Millie sat up, elbows on the old church floor and head cocked to the side. She watched it all happen, the uproar, and it dawned on her.

These people would never let her be. She would live her days with the church until womanhood began and they would marry her off. Her husband would grow something inside of her like all men did and she'd end up like her mother. Raising a child she didn't love. Millie was ten, and she knew all this to be true.

Is it time? Millie asked. *Is it finally time?*

Yeah, kiddo. Have at it, it replied.

Perhaps the resolve showed on her face, or William could also make magic happen, but that boy somehow knew, and above the roar of the church he screamed, "She's gonna make that magic happen!"

He was right.

They All Dead

She killed William first. That stupid, cruel boy with his stupid chubby cheeks and grubby grabbing fingers. She twisted her outstretched hand, his head followed her will and promptly snapped. William fell back in the pew, eyes going milky. Millie picked herself up as the praise turned to screams and William's father shook his boy's empty body. She dusted off her clothes. She turned to Pastor who dunked the rest of the holy water on her. Millie frowned and threw Pastor against the cross nailed behind the podium with the jerk of her arm. She then willed the floor beneath the woman who held her to open up and it swallowed her whole. The floor closed just as her neck passed through, leaving the severed head to bleed out by the altar.

This wine will be my blood, it mocked.

Millie turned. Townspeople were rushing toward the church doors, pulling at the handles which she sealed with a thought. They clawed, nails breaking against the wood, splinters crucifying their fingertips.

"Please, please!" someone screamed.

Millie brought the ceiling down atop the crowd. It crashed with a cloud of sawdust and bodily fluids oozed from under the debris. Millie remained safe, the destruction a wreath around her.

"Hm," she looked around, cocking her head to the side. "They all dead."

Good girl.

A pair of hands tore through the rubble. Millie watched their skin tear as it caught on nails and fresh blood sputtered out. She waited until they heaved themselves out before she approached them. Millie could not tell who this was, their face was punched in and covered in blood. A veil.

Something splattered from their mouth as they attempted to speak and Millie walked over them. She cascaded the rubble wall, picking debris off her good blouse.

Where to now? she asked.

Anywhere, I suppose. But you ought to purge the rest of the town before we go. Millie squinted out at the houses all puffing smoke from their chimneys. A gust of wind blew against her back, a message from a god, maybe. The wind led her forward, and her steps ran loud and clear over the creaking of the church behind her.

About the author
Gail Schoepple has been writing novels and stories since the 8th grade. She is now a writer and graduate student from Moravian University, majoring in English with a Writing Certificate. She works at the oldest bookshop in America and she lives in Allentown, PA.

Part of the Story

Fiona Ritchie Walker

There's something on the floor, moving. Vicky can see it out of the corner of her eye, reflected in the silver curve of the bathroom bin. She is brushing her teeth when the soft flutter catches her attention. She turns to look. A tiny feather.

This time last year the town was full of feathers and the arrival of the gulls made headline news. So did Vicky's story about the film festival cancelling the outdoor showing of *The Birds*. The organisers said it was too soon after the old man had been attacked, after he lay in a hospital bed for three days, with his dodgy heart and pecked skin, then stopped breathing.

Vicky knows a lot about gulls. She's had to learn, look them up on the internet. Background knowledge, that's what helps her write a good story, what gave her voice confidence when Radio 4 asked for an interview.

A bloke who studied journalism with her Tweeted that she was a jammy sod, landing her job on the local paper just weeks before the gull story broke. She'd been in her attic flat ten days when the birds took over the town, slicing through the country air with their razor cries, wide wings skimming heads in narrow streets and alleys, sending children running for their classroom after two swooped in through an open window.

Vicky hated when it all calmed down. After the eggs hatched and the gulls with their nursery flocks flew to the coast, it was empty nests and boredom. She had yawned her way through too many long council meetings, written up heated debates about yellow lines, unemptied recycling bins.

But now the days are brightening, warming. People are talking about the birds again – will they, won't they return? Last week her story about the council's views on dummy eggs, cherry pickers, the possibility of even using hawks was the front page lead. And she got the exclusive about the hotline for locals to call as soon as they see mating pairs, the start of nesting.

Next week it's the anniversary of the gulls flying so far inland, and Jim, the editor, has asked Vicky to write the two-page, pull-out feature. She reads it again, tweaks a few words, pays attention to how it sounds out loud. Last year she missed out on the region's Young Journalist of the Year – pipped at the post was how the judges described it. She won't let it happen again.

Vicky thinks she didn't win because for so many weeks, she was part of the story. When she signed the lease for the flat, it was only because it was cheap and there was nearby parking. She'd not given a thought to location, stuck between the factory and the back of the hotel kitchen with all those tempting bins and scraps in the alley below. The perfect place for gulls to nest, next to her sloping bathroom window. She didn't know that dropping stones was part of a seagull's mating display, until the glass shards tumbled down, splashed up bubbles in her bath.

She was amazed at the lack of pain from such cleanly sliced skin. So much blood. Vicky became her very own story. Picked up by the dailies, nationals and radio too. All in all, a nice little earner. She's tried to keep in touch with some of the bigger names. This time next year she could be with the BBC, Sky, or in London, writing her own column. Who knows? She'll have done her time in this place, will be ready to move on.

Vicky gets a coffee, reads the feature again. It's finished, but she won't let Jim know yet. She doesn't want to spend her day in court, yawning through who's been caught speeding or found urinating in a public place. Let Jim send Andy. He's got a cushy enough job doing all the sport that he'd pay to see anyway.

Last year, after a morning in the local library's archive – avoiding court yet again – Vicky wrote an article about gull folklore, listed so many answers to the question, *did you know?* That some people watch gulls to predict the weather while others say gulls are foolish, "gullible". That gulls stamp their feet, trick earthworms into becoming dinner by thinking there is rain. So many curses and legends too. Maybe she could do a follow-up, All About Gulls, Part Two.

She's just starting a search on the internet when the phone rings. So much crying, Vicky can hardly hear what the woman's saying. But the words *gull* and *puppy* have her reaching for her car keys, heading out the door.

Jim cancels his caravanning holiday the next day. He can't leave Vicky and Andy when it's started up again. The nationals are covering it. Everyone asking, what makes this town the target? By the weekend, so many gulls are flying in they look like a dirty rag trying to clean the clouded sky.

Vicky stops eating in the flat. She's frightened she might miss out, orders pub meals, listens in on conversations. She likes to see if she can spot the strangers, decides visiting media people stand out a mile.

It's when she's leaving The Crown just before closing time that she sees him, a man walking through the park, his steady footsteps startling birds out of trees, stirring up gulls from rooftops. It makes her think of the magnetic game she had when she was little, plastic ladybirds that never met, the dark circles beneath them sending out something invisible, repelling.

Vicky walks more quickly, trying to catch up, hears a

door open, shut. A car drives off down the straight road that leads out of town. On either side, birds shriek and rise, fly off, don't come back.

She has to find out who he is, knows that somehow he's part of her story. She doesn't have a number plate or even a make of car. But he's tall, wild hair tied back. Dressed in thick jacket, scarf, boots, on a warm evening when everyone else is in T-shirts, short sleeves. It should be easy in a town this small, but no-one seems to know him.

The next morning Vicky's sitting at her desk, chewing on a pen, wondering what to do next when there's a call from reception. Will she come down? He's got his back to her when she opens the door to the interview room, sees the jacket, ponytail.

Vicky writes it all down in her notebook. He's read her stories online, followed her on social media, knows she saw the birds disappear from his path. She can be the go-between. Fifty thousand pounds to rid the town of gulls.

By the next morning, Vicky is back to being part of the story, interviewed for breakfast news. Hours after its broadcast, the town has crowdsourced all the money it needs to pay the mysterious stranger, everyone desperate to feel safe again.

He's got conditions. No interviews or name, no photographs or recordings. A room and food, expenses paid, that's all. Vicky visits the empty hotel room with the photographer. She sits on the single chair, poses with her notebook. Not the photo she wanted, but at least it's something.

As agreed, she leaves the hotel, stands at a safe distance outside, no phones or cameras, watches his silhouette walk through the hotel side door, then disappear. She gets into her car and waits. Only when the sun has almost disappeared does he enter the empty street.

114

People watch from crowded windows. Too close and he'll abandon the town to the gulls, to cars with splatted windscreens every morning, children and dogs attacked on their way to school, but the locals find it hard to stay far away. They want to see it for themselves, be able to tell their grandchildren.

He walks slowly, looks straight ahead, wears dark glasses even though the sun has gone. Above him birds abandon nests as he approaches, they circle round, call into the darkening sky. He walks in silence, hands in pockets, doesn't look at the chaos above. An hour later, he's back in his room, food delivered, a jug of black coffee and then the door locked. He doesn't order breakfast, doesn't appear until the same time the following evening. When a woman with a phone steps close, he stares until she shrinks back, puts the mobile in her pocket, turns to walk away.

After five nights every gull, blackbird, sparrow has flown. Eggs grow cold, nests are abandoned. Sky and trees are empty, silent. He's fulfilled his part of the bargain, will be leaving the next morning.

But it can't stop there. Not for Vicky. Someone else will find out why, they'll steal the end of her story. What is this strange gift he has? Was it learned or inherited? She has to know the secret, rings his mobile, which he warned would be dead as soon as he leaves town, feels her heart race when he answers.

A long pause. She can hear him sighing. There are conditions. No notebook, no recorder, just one drink together before he moves on. She replies, waits. Only when he says time and venue does she realise she's been holding her breath.

Vicky takes a bottle and two glasses, drives to the river, finds him watching the water. There's a fish twitching on the bank beside him. She doesn't ask.

If he added once upon a time to his story or said it took place on another planet she might believe him. By the time the bottle's empty, she's sure he's telling her lies. Some other answer must exist, not this nonsense he's saying to try to convince her. He must be saving the truth for the highest bidder.

So don't believe it, he says, but she needs to know. Opens the boot, brings back another bottle. It's her that instigates the first kiss, salty like the sea or maybe tears, leads him to the back of her car. Are you sure, he whispers, slipping his hand inside her shirt. She doesn't stop him. His nails graze her thigh. Afterwards, when he's driven off and the night is silent, she dozes in the car, wakes thinking her heartbeat is the sound of wings.

There's something on the floor, moving, just as there is most mornings now. Vicky can see the feather out of the corner of her eye, reflected in the silver curve of the bathroom bin. She was brushing her teeth, thinking about legends, curses. What to believe. She was wondering about what the man said, where he is now. If he was right, birds will be sitting peacefully in trees above him, his shirt might be open, revealing smooth, bare skin for the first time.

Vicky thinks of the story he told her. The birds killed by a young boy so long ago and now this, passed down through the generations. She believed none of it, but had to find out, told herself a good reporter never gives up on the gift of an exclusive.

To begin with, she could pluck the fresh feathers each morning, but now the quills are lodging firmly in her skin. All her low cut tops still hang at the back of the wardrobe. Jim and Andy have started asking why she's wearing so many layers and scarves when the weather's turned so warm.

Vicky's recording it all in a video diary. Every time she makes another entry, she imagines it as part of a documentary. There will be a bidding war, she thinks. With the man at the heart of the story gone, it's all hers now. Book, film, interviews. It should set her up nicely.

There's a flurry of wings above the skylight window. When she looks up, a pigeon – rare in the town these days – shrieks and flaps against the glass, veers away. Another feather, pale and soft, escapes from the folds of her dressing gown. Vicky bends to pick it up, gasps. Deep in her belly there's a fluttering.

About the author

Fiona Ritchie Walker is a Scottish writer, now based in England. For many years she travelled the world visiting fair trade artisans and farmers to help them share their stories. Her poetry and short fiction has been widely published, most recently in *Amsterdam Quarterly*, Scotland's *Postbox Magazine* and Bristol University's anthology *Secret Life of Data*.

www.fionaritchiewalker.com

Strictly Most Haunted

Julia Wood

It's four o'clock in the morning, not quite night-time but not yet light. There's no one else in my carriage, so I should try and sleep but I'm not tired enough. Intermittently the faded yellow strip light above me buzzes and flickers, which irritates me.

I pick up my plastic glass of wine and take a big gulp. I'm on Mini Bottle Number Two already and we only left Market Harborough fifteen minutes ago. God knows what the woman behind the counter must have thought of me asking for five mini bottles, and at four in the morning. People's expectations. That's what makes me hit the wine.

Resolution took a long time. That's how it is sometimes. They reach out, they want to connect. They need me to stay, drinking coffee and talking into the early hours, reassuring them everything will be okay. That's how it was with Darrell too. So, I did some walking around, closing my eyes, until I could feel the sadness in the air. Then I told her about the young maid who'd lived there in the Victorian age and had cried herself to sleep because she was lonely and had no one to love.

It's narratives people need. Narratives that help them make sense of the unfathomable, of death. I need them too. That's how I got into all this – in pursuit of meaningful narratives. I don't get paid for it. In fact, I'm currently "between jobs", which is the middle-class term for unemployed. I wanted to be a dancer. I still do, but at fifty-six, I'm too old. Besides, I'm not talented enough. Hey ho.

Several miles of rattling through open countryside later, the train stops. The strip light buzzes and flickers again and two sets of familiar elderly couples get in. I only catch a glimpse of them, arms linked, huddled together, as they get

118

into the carriage in front of me. I'm just trying to compute my sense of déjà vu when my attention is diverted by a hippie-looking woman with blue hair and multiple piercings.

"Is it okay if I sit here?" she says.

A part of me is relieved to have company; another part of me wonders why she doesn't sit somewhere else when the rest of this carriage is empty.

"Yes, of course," I reply because I'm too tired to challenge her and besides, it might put off any weird blokes that may head my way.

She takes the seat opposite me, stares at me. The wine makes me braver, so I stare back. I notice her soft skin, the fine lines setting in around her eyes, her small, slight frame. Mid-forties, I would guess.

"You're lost," she says in a voice that sounds like she's doing a guided meditation. "You're on the wrong journey."

"No, I'm not," I reply. "This *is* the London train."

She raises a pierced brow. The tiny silver stud reminds me of those hundreds-and-thousands on my childhood birthday cake, when the world was still a magical exciting place, and anything was possible.

"Life journey," she says, as if this is perfectly normal thing to be telling a total stranger on a train in the small hours.

I frown, feeling vulnerable and edgy. I squeeze my hand around my glass until a small crack appears in the plastic.

"You took a wrong turn, Clarissa. Way back."

How does she know my name? I contemplate getting up and going to sit somewhere else, but, woozy and tired as I am, I stay put.

"Mediumship is not your true calling."

I tap my heel against the radiator nervously, trying to recall if I told her that just now, but my head is thick with exhaustion and alcohol, and I can't think straight.

"Your talents lie elsewhere."

"Where are you getting all this from?"

"It's what they're telling me."

"They?" I watch her for a moment, then I understand.

"You don't remember me, do you?"

I shake my head. "Should I?"

"Spiritual development circle? Nineteen-ninety-nine?"

"That's going back some. I'm afraid I don't."

"I'm Shauna. I sat next to you. I only came to a couple of meetings, then I... I gave it up." She holds out her hand.

I don't reciprocate. She withdraws it, looking hurt, but I'm confused and disoriented, trying to figure out why someone I only met twice over two decades ago would remember me by name.

"I'm sorry if I've offended you. I just get this stuff coming through, and I have to tell people."

"It's okay. It's just... since Covid, you know. You can't be too careful." I glance at my bag at the side of me, the packet of sanitizers sticking up. I close the zip, feeling myself blush. I don't have an excuse. I'm just uncomfortable with the attention.

"You really helped me back then," she says. "You were the only one who gave me any decent advice. The others kept telling me how talented I was and how I mustn't block those that want to come through. You know, never mind if it's giving me a frigging breakdown." She rolls her eyes.

"Sorry, it was a long time ago. What... what advice did I give you?"

"I was struggling with my psychic ability. I'd had psychologists on my case, saying I was mad, wanting to section me. They wouldn't leave me alone. Spirits, I mean, not psychologists." She manages a smile. "You just said, 'Tell them to do one,' something like that."

"Did I?" It's my turn to smile.

"Then you said I had to fold my arms because I needed to say *bog off* with my body language too."

I manage a laugh. "Did it work?"

"Eventually. I mean, I was, like, twenty. I just wanted to go to the pub with my mates and get drunk, but I'd see all these dead people drifting around the fruit machine." She glances at the row of bottles.

She thinks she's got me nailed, but she hasn't, because that's not it. I don't drink to blot out what I've seen. That's not why I'm getting wasted on the 4.04 to London St. Pancras by myself.

"I just wanted a *normal* life. And you helped me achieve that. It's thanks to you I've been able to manage my ability, tune it out when I want a break."

"I'm glad I could help you." I'm used to people confiding in me, asking me for advice, for readings. The *can-you-see-my-gran-who-died-last-Wednesday* kind of readings. It's all part of the deal when people find out you're a medium. But this? It's surreal.

I look out of the window, at the in-between-times sky, watching the rose-coloured, ethereal light creeping in, listening to the rhythmic rattle of the train. It pulls into another station, stops with a squeak of brakes and waits. The strip light buzzes, flickers, buzzes, flickers its irritating rhythm. Something reflected behind me unnerves me. A flash of red floaty dress, a mass of long hair. I whip my gaze round, to the inside of the carriage, but it's still empty. I shake my head like I'm trying to ward off a wasp. I return my gaze to the window as the train pulls off. The only reflection I can see is my own navy-blue puffer, my own scribble of unbrushed hair. I begin to wonder if I'm going a bit mad.

"What's the most haunted place you've ever been in?"

I slug back the rest of my wine, the rush of acidity making me cough.

"That would be telling." *My mind,* I think to myself, *my mind.*

The train pulls off again. The Tannoy, softly spoken as a night nurse, welcomes the *just-joined-this-train* passengers.

"You didn't always want to be a medium," she says.

It's a statement, not a question.

"I mean, since you were a child."

Clearly, she's not giving up. I've run out of Cabernet Sauvignon, so I open Mini Bottle Number Four – the Chardonnay – and pour it into the stemmed plastic glass. I run my finger around the rim, hoping she'll get off at the next stop.

"No," I reply. "I didn't." I take a big gulp from my Chardonnay. It tastes like drain cleaner. I wince.

"Mediumship – it's a calling, a vocation. It chooses you; you don't choose it."

I did, I think to myself.

As if to illustrate her point, Shauna closes her eyes and turns her palms upwards.

"I'm getting a deep sadness." She pauses, opens her eyes and puts her hands on top of mine. "Someone dear to you *passed into spirit.*" She says *passed into spirit* in a voice so soft it's like a ghost has wafted through the carriage. "You… you lost *a half of yourself* that day."

I sit, paralysed with an emotion somewhere between dread and anticipation.

The train stops again. No one seems to be getting on, or off. After a while the doors close with a muted thump, and it moves on.

"She's still here," Shauna says. "She's with you… all the time. She says it happened so fast, the driver—" She presses a hand to her chest. "Pain. I'm feeling numb, vice in my chest crushing me… folding forward over the wheel;

lorry full of milk… all over the road, oh but 'don't cry over spilt milk, don't cry,' they're saying—"

I let a tear fall; inhibitions vanquished by alcohol.

"She used to get mad at you for beating her at tennis… she says… 'I know you let me win that time on holiday in Ibiza.' "

I listen, stunned at how her voice changes and she sounds like Clare; has Clare's quirky way of enunciating the word *Eye*-beetha, with the emphasis on the first part of the word.

"She's giving me the colour red. She says, 'Wear red, it makes me feel closer.' It was your favourite colour – yours and hers."

I nod, stunned. "I don't understand how a connection so strong can suddenly break." I take a shaky breath. "I was at home when it happened. I felt the impact. When you're a twin it's like you're one person." I wipe away a tear. "I kept her photo by my bed. I talked to her every day, wrote her letters." My head is starting to ache, from tiredness or the wine, I'm not sure. "I've spent my life trying… trying to find it again, just wanting there to be something… hoping. I'm not—" I stop myself. Even drunk I'm not sure I can say this.

"You're not what?"

"I… *do* try. I try so hard. I want to help people."

"I know you do."

"But I don't do anything. It's all… *show*."

She stares at me. I look away.

"'I've never—" I take another desperate gulp of wine. "I don't see spirit. I just pretend I do. I'm a *fake, a fraud*." I bite hard on my lip. "I… I don't mean to be."

She doesn't appear shocked, like she already knows this. I've never told anyone. I even lied at the development circle.

123

"Sometimes we do the wrong things for the right reasons. You even believe it yourself. Because you really want to."

"Yes," I admit guiltily, because here I am, wanting to see the very things she'd once asked me for help to stop seeing. "After Clare died, I started trying to train myself to be a psychic – not for money or anything, not like that. I thought maybe I could help to heal others the way I could never heal myself. So, hence the psychic development circle. I was always good at reading atmospheres – I had that kind of intuition going on, comes from being a twin I think. But I never really got further than that, never got actual messages."

She nods knowingly. "You need to let go of the past. Until you do that you will always be trapped in a false identity."

"I contacted loads of mediums to see if she'd come through. I just wanted... I wanted to restore a broken connection – sorry, this sounds like a 'poor me' story. It's the wine, it makes me emotional." I feel guilty for offloading on her, so I change the subject back to her. "But what about you?"

"What about me?"

"You said I helped you manage your talent? But you're here now, giving me a reading."

"I'm here by choice. Some messages you have to pass on. Yours is one of them."

"Oh."

"You have a gift. And you're not using it."

I look out of the window again, but we're entering a tunnel. I feel my ears pop slightly.

"You're twirling and gliding... applause. But I'm sensing heartbreak, disappointment. They're showing me a pair of dancing shoes – and they're on fire. You burnt your

124

dreams. I'm not sure if this is literal or not, but that's what they're showing me."

"I used to want to be a professional dancer." I sigh. "Showbiz. One failed audition too many." I think of my final audition two decades ago, in the West End – the casting call of doom, me in that red floaty dress, trying to fake an enthusiasm I no longer had. "I was twenty-five, young and hopeful. I used to live for dancing. I'd won prizes at school, starred in local shows. It was *world here I come*. But the big bad world turned out to be tougher than I'd imagined. I guess I just didn't have what it takes. But I kept going, because I'd always had Clare cheering me on, believing in me."

"Sounds like you have a few ghosts to exorcise too," she says.

"Yep, I spend my life exorcising other peoples' ghosts while failing miserably to deal with my own. Ironic, huh?" I laugh. "I'd love to be on *Strictly*. But that's not likely to happen."

"That doesn't mean you can't find other opportunities," she says, like it's that simple. "There must be dance groups locally. Shows you could audition for?"

"I've never danced since... Clare."

She puts her hands on mine. "She's saying, 'Go for it.' " There's an urgency in her voice. "Go to night classes, do Am Dram auditions, dance in your room, in the street, at clubs. Promise me."

"I don't know if—"

Her *hundreds-and-thousands* stud lifts up towards a hairline the colour of summer sky. "I'll let you into a secret," she whispers, a glint of mischief in her eye. "I was asked to present a TV show years ago, you know, when the first wave of reality shows hit the screens."

"Really?"

125

"It was a psychic show. They wanted me to go into famous people's houses, give readings, tell them about the ghosts that lived there. *Britain's Most Haunted Celebrities.*" She laughs. "Looking back, it was tacky as hell. But that's not why I turned it down. I was tempted, believe me – be a reality star? Tons of people wanted that in the early noughties. Embarrassing, I know." She rolls her eyes. "But I'd learned to control my ability by then, tune stuff out. I knew if I did it, I'd be inviting it all back in. So, you see, you've helped me. Now it's my turn to help you."

The train judders roughly from side-to-side.

"What was *that*?" I say.

There's another judder. I feel the beginnings of panic. We're still in the tunnel, my gaze goes to the wires and pipes that run along the wall. I fight claustrophobia.

There's a sharp jolt, a squeak of brakes; a crunch of metal, blackness.

I'm travelling fast, down a long starry tunnel; it feels like the night sky has folded itself around me. I can see a brighter light at the end pulling me towards it. Soon, I find myself in a vast, dome-like space with a white shiny floor. There are coloured purple and blue lights. I can hear cheering, but only faintly. *Where am I?*

I extend my gaze over the rest of the space, through the flare of the lights. I'm in the centre of the room. Facing me is a panel of familiar faces, all looking at me. My parents, my grandparents, arms linked, huddled close together.

I look down at myself. I'm in a loose red dress. A figure appears in front of me. She too, is in a red chiffon dress. I watch her gliding towards me. She has my long hair, my dark eyes. She takes my hand. We curl, we twirl, and we glide, we are swans made of flames. As we dance, I mirror her. I *am* her, and she is me.

When we finish there is a cheer from the audience. There is applause, the lights get brighter. Everyone is clapping, my mother cries and smiles. They each hold up a number. *Ten. Ten. Ten. Ten.*

I watch the figure moving closer towards me, dissolving into tiny particles of light that land on my face, my hands, my hair. I feel her energy melting into me, until I am flying through the clouds, up and up.

There's a long bleep. I feel myself being pulled backwards violently. I hit the bed as if fired from a canon. The bleeping stops, replaced with a metronome sound. I open my eyes. Beneath me, the soft white sheets, above me the strip-lights.

A nurse comes in, checks the clipboard pinned to my bed. "It was touch and go for a while, Clarissa but you're going to be okay with plenty of rest. Good to have you back with us."

"How is—" My voice is hoarse and weak.

"Don't try to talk," she says. "Just rest."

"Shauna," I manage. "The girl I was on the train with? We were talking."

"Oh, I'm not sure. Let me see what I can find out for you."

After a few minutes of checking the drip at the side of me she leaves, and I'm left staring at the white plastic curtain around my bed thinking about Shauna and her advice. *Mediumship is not your true calling.* One thing for sure, I can't go back. Not now.

Local auditions. That's what she'd said. I don't just want to dance informally. I want to go back on the stage. Dare I go for it? Doubts swarm in, like tiny ants, but I flick them away. *I just nearly died.* What could possibly be worse than that?

The white plastic curtain parts and the nurse comes back in.

127

"I'm sorry," she says. "There was no one called Shauna on the train."

"What do you mean? I was talking to her I—"

"You were the only passenger on the train when the crash happened."

"But I can't have been, there were others too, two lots of couples, elderly. I thought—"

"There was just you and the driver. The driver didn't make it."

I start to cry.

"You mustn't upset yourself," she says in her bedside voice. "Try and get some sleep." She leaves again, a swish of white curtain falling back into place behind her like a cloud.

I dry my tears on the sleeve of my hospital gown. I know what I have to do. I am ready.

About the author

Julia Wood holds a Masters' Degree in Continental Philosophy from Warwick University and has previously published a non-fiction book, *The Resurrection of Oscar Wilde: A Cultural Afterlife* (Lutterworth Press, 2007). She is a writer of Women's Fiction and short stories, many of which have been anthologised. Her women's fiction/comedy novel, *The Adventures of Jenny Bean, aged 49, and an Awful Lot* was longlisted for the Fiction Factory First Chapter competition (September 2022) and the Yeovil Literary Prize (June, 2023). The sequel novella, *Jenny Bean, Calamity Queen*, was short listed for the CWIP Prize (February 2023) and will be published in *The Book of Witty Women* anthology in September.

She is a longstanding member of Leicester Writers' Club.

Please check out her website at www.julia-wood.com.

The Pattern of Seamie O'Connell

Seamus D Norris

"He's dead and nobody remembers him for what he wanted to be remembered for."

"And what was that?" a voice queried from behind.

I didn't realise I was talking aloud at the mound of clay covering my father's grave with the flower arrangements adorning the freshly shovelled heap. I thought I was alone for my moments of grief with all having dispersed for the tea in the community centre. I turned around sharply, with the fright and some embarrassment. The question disturbed the sombreness of my solitude. It was Philly, Dad's best friend. They kicked Gaelic Football together for many years. Philly was a local hero having played for the county and won a National League medal, the only man from the local club Lambay to do so in the last half century.

I still "fanboyed" Philly, even though he was retired with twenty years. I thought the words of my reply in my head as I stared in awe at Philly, the years had not served him well. The greasy hair on the sides of his skull could have done with a modern makeover. Dad wanted to be a team manager of the club adult team, but he never got the chance. Parish pump politics stifled his ambition. The club had for decades now failed to escape the reputation and consignment of being a mediocre junior team, never to fulfil potential. It hurt Dad, that despite all the lads near and far who got a shot of breaking the never-ending cycle of flattering to deceive, he never got the opportunity to prove his leadership or expose his motivational skills, his knowledge of the game, astute decision making and the brilliance of his people management. His words, not mine. To be honest in my younger years, I didn't realise it either.

Maybe it was his ability to make every piece of advice sound like a teacher's lecture. Combined with my own youthful rebellious streak, it was recipe for stubbornness on my behalf even though I know now with the advantage of hindsight, he was almost always right. I wonder did I tell him. Did he know I was proud to be his son? He wanted to be the best manager he could possibly be by facilitating his players to be the best they can possibly be while unifying the supporters in a spirit of togetherness to achieve county titles and more.

"The greatest team manager ever." The lump in my throat and the tears in my eye adversely affected the clarity of the delivery of my answer. It's cold. I thought that would excuse the emotion. The fact that he had just been buried having died unexpectedly from a cardiac arrest never entered my mind, though the truth was clear.

Philly held out his hand. I took it nervously and shook it. I knew this man so well. Yet even at twenty plus years of age, I was still star struck. "Sorry for your troubles," he said, "Your father was a great man. I will leave you together." He turned to leave me to my mourning. Then he suddenly stopped and said, "Can I tell you a story?"

"Sure," I hesitantly replied.

He began. "When your father and I were young lads, Lambay's Minor Gaelic Footballers were invited to take part in one off Seven-A-Side football match against local rivals Coolbaun as part of the Coolbaun Pattern. A pátrún, in Irish Roman Catholicism refers to the devotions that take place within a parish on the feast day of the patron saint of the parish on that date or the nearest Sunday and was called Pattern Sunday," Philly explained. "Outside the praying, for us it was a Field Day with lots of fun stuff, games and sport."

Our greatest and most hated rivals, Coolbaun, I thought. *Any story involving them and my father should be interesting. Our religion was hating Coolbaun, especially as they were always more successful than Lambay.*

Philly continued. "We were obviously invited not just because we were neighbours but because Coolbaun felt they could beat us easily in front of their own. Who would blame them? Unfortunately, nobody in Lambay wanted to manage us Under-18s. No adult whatsoever! Who wants a minor football team that most likely would be annihilated by their greatest foe for pure entertainment of their own? Gladiators to the slaughter!

"Seamie O'Connell was having none of it. Your father roped me into helping him. He said he needed me as the selling point. He said if our best player was in, the others will follow. I was chuffed and delighted he said it. We set about getting seven lads to play. The odds were stacked against us. It wasn't easy but we somehow got seven aces, lads we grew up with. We were ready, kind of. We had no ball of our own for the warm up. No water, no first aid and barely got the jerseys. I think only some of our parents came to support us in Coolbaun. The seven were Seanie Kelleher, Eamonn McDonagh, Jimmy Kinsella, Dinny Flynn, Simon Brogan, your father and myself who were joint player managers. Seamie was also Captain and to be honest, he was the real leader. The only leader. I was just a figurehead. We were like 'The Magnificent Seven' heading to Coolbaun. Seamie and myself were like Yul Brynner and Steve McQueen! We arrived in Coolbaun on the back of my Honda 50, barely room for the plastic gear bags which just had the boots in. Some team bus all the same. I cannot recollect how the other five lads got there." Philly was building up the story with his reference to Westerns. Dad loved Westerns too.

"Analysis of the situation with a view to a solution was Seamie's mantra," Philly continued. "He studied our strengths and although he didn't get it fully right starting off, he switched us around to get the best from the team. We trailed one goal and one point to a goal at half time. Simon got our goal. The partisan crowd were delighted to be leading at the break although they must have been surprised we were so close. We even heard men from Coolbaun laughing that we had nobody managing us except ourselves. A bunch of young galoots they thought we were. Seamie started as a forward, but he was not making any impression despite working his socks off. Seamie was not the most skilful player but without a shadow of a doubt he was the fittest and hardest working player who ever played for Lambay. I started at midfield. I was never as fit as your dad, but I knew I could do well closer to the goal. Seamie switched me and he went lár na páirce."

That made sense to me. Philly Waters was a super forward playing for the county team. I could sense the enthusiasm in Philly's story. I had just buried my father and suddenly and inexplicably Philly's story started to excite me.

Philly continued. "At half time, any confidence we had was ebbing with the increased mocking from the local supporters. Your dad, looked at us. Then he stared momentarily at the old guys from Coolbaun. Then he turned and spoke to us. Remember, he was not yet eighteen years of age and this is the gist of what he said. My friends, this is about belief in what we can do. We've got to believe we can beat these lads. We cannot stop believing in our own ability. But we've got to be intelligent in how we go about it. We must use the ball wisely. We have to respect the ability of the opposition, even though we hate them and want so much to beat them off the field. We have to trust our own ability and the ability of each other and most of all, we have to be honest. Honest to each other and honest to ourselves. We have to give every ounce of energy for each other and for Lambay. Lambay deserted us. We will not dessert Lambay! We will make Lambay proud!"

Philly's retelling of my father's oration made the hairs stand on the back of my neck. For a brief moment I felt Dad standing next to us, delivering the words with gusto and passion.

Philly continued. "We ran back on to that pitch with a spring in our step. My own father was one of the few there. I wanted to make him proud. We all wanted to make somebody proud. At that moment this was our All-Ireland Final. A mere Minor seven-a-side game in a country field with made up goal posts and loads of sideshows going on around from tossing the sheaf to fishing for bottles of minerals to skittles to milking an artificial cow. Not a prayer to be heard except the ones within our minds as we prayed to God we could win the game for Lambay.

Coolbaun got another early goal at the start of the second half. I thought that was that. The oul fellas were having a field day, pardon the pun. Seamie still believed we could win. As Seamie the player, he worked harder. As Seamie, Manager and Captain, he shouted louder and prouder. There was nothing in mind and body that he was going to leave on that pitch. His actions inspired us all. Now we wanted to do it for him. Then he reminded us of something very important. After he put in a huge block where he put his body on the line, he roared; if you are not going to do it for Lambay, do it for yourself! Make yourself proud!

I gave it my all and set up Simon for a second goal. We were a point down. With a minute to go Seamie won a "dirty" ball at midfield, played a quick accurate pass to me.

It was so sweet. I burst through the Coolbaun cover and drilled the ball to the back of the net. It was an amazing feeling. The partisan crowd were stunned into silence especially the Statler and Waldorf of Coolbaun. Lambay won by two points, three goals to 2-1. It was unbelievable, but true. I have the medal to this day and it is one of my most prized medals. The seven of us celebrated like Riverdancers. Seamie accepted the cup and you never saw such a prouder beaming smile. He said, Lambay, this is for you all. We are the greatest! This is just the beginning. That day inspired me to want that feeling of euphoria over and over again. It was like a drug. When I think back, I don't think winning the National League medal felt as good. Your dad was the best friend and the greatest manager I ever played for and with."

Philly concluded his story. My mouth was ajar. My tears of sadness were replaced with tears of joy and pride. Pride in my father, Seamie O'Connell.

"So you see young, Shay," Philly looked me in the eye and took a firm grip of my hand while placing the other on my shoulder, "does it matter how many people remember? I don't think so, as long as someone remembers. I remember Seamie O'Connell as the greatest manager. A gifted and talented manager that would have been a tremendous asset no matter what the sport or business for that matter. When I'm gone, you will too and so will anyone who hears the story of the 1980 Pattern of Coolbaun. Again, sorry for your troubles. Take care and be proud of yourself and what you do."

At that, Philly turned and limped away, his hips showing the wear and tear of his sporting endeavours. That's what a sympathiser does at an Irish funeral. I turned and looked at Dad's grave, happy to know he was remembered as the greatest Bainisteoir by at least one person and at least one person would remember him as the greatest dad. Maybe the Pattern of Seamie O'Connell is something to celebrate.

About the author

Seamus D Norris is an Irish Business Analyst and Gaelic Games enthusiast, but he is also a keen storyteller. His stories come from his exciting and vivid imagination, mainly revolving around Sport, Westerns, Romance and Crime or are Irish themed, based on dramatised versions of his own life experiences. The stories range from drama to comedy, and he uses multiple platforms of novels, novellas, plays of all lengths, short stories, poetry and song lyrics to tell interesting and important stories.

Seamus has had short stories and poetry published, song lyrics for a song that reached a national song contest final, one-act plays performed in the Macra Na Feirme drama competition, rehearsed readings by drama groups/well-known directors, and, during the COVID lockdown, a short play streamed by Barnstorm Theatre Arts.

His motto is "Dreams and ambitions have no Limit", but it is not riches he seeks, just for as many people around the world as is possible to hear or see his stories.

The Pudding Cake

Adjie Henderson

Winter had barely come, but the weather was cold, dreary and tiresome. Too much snow had fallen and the winds had blown the snow into almost impassable piles. Janet sat quietly watching it all from the window in her warm house. She was tired and didn't plan to leave her comfortable old chair any time soon. She had spent days throwing away stuff she no longer needed. The Swedes call it döstädning or perhaps in her more concise definition, she was doing premortem cleaning. Janet had no plans to die, but in the event she did, she didn't want her children to spend their valuable time sorting through the mess of her old professional papers, books, and unidentifiable family portraits. At the top of a book pile for discard was her high school yearbook. She flicked through the yellowing pages and noted that the ink of the optimistic handwritten notes inside the front cover was fading and it smelled of old book.

The messages from friends were pretty much the same and all optimistic, like, "You will go into the world and change it forever; we will be friends always, love and kisses, Babette."

Suddenly she was overcome with a mild form of empathic guilt.

"I must visit Babette," she thought. "I should've gone a long time ago, but a visit is so depressing."

They were always together when they were young. Even then, Babette was different from the other children. Most retained some portions of childhood as they dealt with puberty, but not Babette. She was always an adult. Her long black hair was in a fashionable do, not a cheap cut from the local beautician. Later, she had dates, real exotic dates, in gorgeous dresses and high heels. As they entered their teen years, Babette saw Janet with fond memories, but like an old shoe, already assigned to the rear of a closet.

After Law School, Janet married and later divorced, a fellow Law student, a comfortable guy who moved with her into her parent's old house. Babette married a famous college football star she was dating in high school, an event that was most impressive for the more mortal students. The women met sporadically in the years that followed. Recently, a common friend mentioned Babette's current address. She lived on the other side of town now in an area long forgotten or dismissed by most of the town's people.

"I will take her present – her favourite cake," Janet said aloud. "Her life is a lazy drunk husband. It's very depressing. According to gossip, he sits in front of the TV in his jockeys and a dirty old T-shirt, company or not. He always frightens me."

The cake she constructed was magnificent with coconut frosting and chocolate pudding between the layers. No one answered when she phoned earlier to announce her arrival, but then Babette seldom answered. If no one was home, she was going for a bruschetta and a nice wine for herself at a local restaurant. Maybe she would go anyway.

She saw the house in her mind even before she arrived and mentally prepared to leave the cake on a broken-down porch. Indeed, the porch needed paint and a chainsaw leaning against a railing holding uncut wood formed the only decorative touch. She could creep away to the restaurant bar, but the house had half-open doors caused by the frenetic movement of people in the same suit. She introduced herself to one of the suits who turned out to be a local detective.

"What in god's holy name is going on here?" she asked, but no one answered.

"I don't know who you are and we will question you sooner or later. Please sit down and wait. Do not touch anything."

She sat quietly in the assigned chair, her cake box in her lap. The room was dark. The only light was a ray of dusty sunshine in the kitchen. Gradually her eyes acclimatized to the dimness and she saw Babette sitting in the corner on an old couch. She didn't speak. She just sat there; her hands folded in her lap.

"What is happening?" Janet asked, holding Babette's cold hands.

There was no reply from the huddled figure. Babette didn't look up but wrapped herself more tightly in a dirty old blanket.

"Babette, what is happening?"

There was a moan but no voice. She sat quietly in an old, faded house dress and bedroom shoes as if waiting for something.

""How well do you know the suspect?" asked one of the detectives.

"Suspect," Janet said, "What are you talking about?"

"Someone killed her husband," he said, "and she was the only person here. We can't find any evidence of a forced entry and the snoopy neighbours didn't see anyone enter or leave the house. He was killed this morning. The neighbours called us."

Janet suggested to a female detective that they go with Babette for a change of clothes. As they helped her wash, it was obvious that she had been badly beaten. Janet and the detective looked with disbelief. The back of Babette's gown was bloody, as was the bed. After the detective made photographs, they got her dressed. She refused to be taken to the emergency room.

Babette was now old. Her breasts sagged, her ankles

were swollen and her beautiful hair was badly cut as if done by her own scissors. Her ears were larger and her nose was another victim of gravity. The face Janet first saw in the dark was the face in the high school yearbook, not the wrinkled face that was really there. Janet realized now that when she looked in the mirror herself, it was not the high school girl of the yearbook. She was also grey, wrinkled and tired. Age is a levelling ground.

"If she killed him, it was self-defence," Janet offered. "He was a rough crappy guy who virtually held her captive here. How do you know it was her? Anyone could have come in – a burglar, an enemy, a stranger disenchanted with the world. Maybe the snoopy neighbours missed this during a quick trip to the toilet. On another note, would you like a piece of cake? I brought it for her. Perhaps she could eat something?"

"The neighbours heard her screaming… *I am going to kill you*... and we found her note that admitted she'd killed him. It doesn't look good. Everyone believes her husband was god's gift to the neighbourhood. Apparently he spent his time with the local boys who adore him and his tales of football prowess."

"Do you know where the gun is?" the detective asked.

"Of course not," Janet replied, "I didn't know they had a gun. Believe me, he was an asshole. Can I go to the kitchen and slice some cake?"

"OK, but don't touch anything,"

"Just a rubber spatula. I mean if I can't use a knife."

"Don't use a knife," the young female detective directed, although she did not really believe this sweet little old lady would run around the house waving a kitchen knife.

The female detective watched her for a moment as she tried to reconstruct the layers of the cake with a spatula and then went back to work trying to find possible evidence.

"Let's keep the old lady here for a while to determine if she knows anything." said the head detective within hearing range. "Perhaps she can coax some info from Babette. Then she can take her freaking cake and go home. Get her name and address."

Babette sat in the same spot on the couch. She didn't touch her cake, but the detectives had a slice. Janet went to the kitchen and noticed the piles of dirty dishes in the sink and set about cleaning up. She knew they would take Babette away for questioning and probably keep her. This group was too far into showing what they perceived as their outstanding detection skills. Some preparations were necessary in case she could ever come home. As she cleaned she remembered their childhood, playing in a cardboard box in the back yard... windows and doors drawn in vivid colours with crayons. They pretended they would grow up and marry important men and all live together and love the world in the house with crayon window boxes.

She put everything perishable in the refrigerator and then in an afterthought, she checked the oven. She found a dirty pot containing beans.

"Why on earth would you put beans in the oven in a stovetop pot?" Janet asked the mute figure sitting on the couch watching her.

Looking into the messy pot, Janet noticed that the beans didn't have a smooth top surface. The gun was in the beans. Janet looked around and then picked the gun out of the beans with an old dishcloth. She looked at Babette and remembered the King Cake at Epiphany and the game they played as children – what could you hide in a cake? Then she removed the top layer of the remaining cake, put the gun inside between the layers holding the chocolate pudding and redecorated the icing. She knew that without a gun, there would be problems with their proving her guilt. In any case, things would move along more quickly.

"Are you still futzing with the cake?" asked a detective checking on her activities.

"Finished," she said. "When can I leave?"

"We are taking Babette in now" he said. "Please leave enough information for us to find you if necessary."

Janet waited on the porch for them to take her away. Babette turned and looked at her. Perhaps she smiled. Janet got back on the crosstown bus carrying the rest of the cake wrapped in a plastic shopping bag. She had never done a criminal act before and sat with a mixture of fear and excitement, watching to see if anyone recognized her. When she got to her stop, she handed the bag to one of the sanitation guys collecting garbage who tossed it into the steaming mass in the rear of the truck. Janet, the criminal lawyer and advisor to the police detective division, came home to sit in her comfy chair and have a stiff scotch.

About the author
Adjie Henderson is a scientist and previously a Dean for Graduate Sciences. She has published over two hundred articles on diverse research topics, from molecular genetics to setting standards for environmental controls. Her current activities are concentrated on restoring the environment. She has published many short stories, none of which have to do with the credentials above.

The Road to Success Is Always under Construction

Athena Constantinou

As a little girl, I was passionate about making up stories, which I later told to anyone who would listen. While most children my age helped their parents with the housework, I spent my time outdoors, writing my ideas on little pieces of paper and turning them into stories to tell to my audience.

Although my father was an uneducated man, he firmly believed that knowledge was important for the progress of society, and he constantly urged me to go to university one day. "As long as you work hard at school, you do not have to work on the farm," he said, and he did not even allow my mother to bother me with chores. "Alison will be great one day, and great minds should not waste their time doing dishes," he said insistently, and then would hurry off to help my mother with everything, which added to his long hours of work, as long as I was not disturbed. And my mother also wanted only the best for her little girl. With a pantry filled only with bags of rice, lentils, and trahana – a kind of dry food based on a mixture of ground wheat and fermented milk – she prepared the kind of meals that made me feel like a queen. And when she called me "my little princess", I believed it to be true. My childhood was not particularly carefree; in fact, it was difficult. But I was happy because I was loved. And for a young girl who had experienced so much love, this happiness was quite enough.

So the years went by without me having to worry about anything, except school. I had never really understood how hard life was on a farm, because my father did his best to take care of me. Still, I kept up my end of the bargain by

142

bringing home top grades and making my father proud during his school visits.

And then the day came when I was to go to the best private high school in the city, for I had won a scholarship. But my excitement about the new school quickly died down when I realised that I was in a class where all my classmates wore freshly starched shirts, trousers, and skirts that came from stores I had never been to. And the constant chatter from my classmates about their parents' office jobs in the city, their new cars, and their vacations to places I could not even find on a map, let alone visit, left me feeling disoriented and confused. For the first time in my life, I could not ignore the loud pounding of my heart, the heat in my face, and the trembling in my hand as I had to explain that my father was a farmer and our home was a stone house on the outskirts of town.

I had always known that the clothes I wore and the toys I played with came from the other children in the village, and I had never forgotten the frequent knock at the door followed by the two words I hated but wanted to hear at the same time – "for Alison". And how the privileged women of the village would discreetly place their bundles on the doorstep, politely decline my mother's request to come in and taste her freshly baked cake, and then leave with a satisfied smile on their lips, because they had done what they considered their duty to God and society. Nevertheless, I was happy during that time because my parents had taught me to be grateful for the simple things in life.

Still, this humble life in our weather-beaten stone house on the outskirts of town, its roof collapsing and held together only by pieced-together pieces of wood and metal, was all I knew. So I only became aware of my family's poverty when I went to private school and had to deal with kids who had a very different background from mine. I was not ashamed of my family. On the contrary. I was proud of my parents. But despite my success in school and the praise of my teachers, I became increasingly angry at my classmates who made fun of my life on the farm, at society for being unfair, and sometimes at my parents for not being upset by this injustice. "Money is not everything," they would say in unison when I confronted them with these issues that plagued me.

One day, after a heated argument with one of my classmates, I ran home after school and tearfully asked my parents why they always had to work so hard, but they didn't answer and just looked at me lovingly. My mother took me tenderly in her arms, dried my wet cheeks, silenced my sobbing lips, while my father stroked my long brown hair. "Wealth isn't measured in money, and money alone isn't enough to make you happy. This injustice, as you call it, is simply the way of the world," they explained, and went on to describe how some people are born rich, others become rich through hard work, and how others have to work hard just to have enough. But they also clarified that nothing in life is predetermined and that everyone can change what they don't like and create their own destiny. So I shouldn't cry, but instead focus on how I want to shape my life. "The road to success is always under construction," my father would emphasise. And above all, I should not feel sad for them because they were content with their lives and the work on the farm was not so hard. And when my father held my hand and I felt the blisters on his palm, I realised that hands are always more honest than faces.

The next day my father came home with his usual smile. "I have a gift for you that I think will help you get in life what I believe you deserve," he said, handing me a brown leather-bound notebook and a smooth and voluminous silver fountain pen that was curved at the top so it would fit better in my hand. Both expensive gifts, purchased with my parents' modest savings that had taken years to build up and my mother referred to as our emergency fund. "From now on, I want you to write down the beautiful stories that always made us so happy when you told them to us, before the world takes away your love of writing, your beautiful smile and the sparkle in your eyes. In a time of sadness, your stories will remind you of who you really are, while the rest of the world will try to tell you who they want you to be. And maybe one day you'll be able to share those stories with the world and bring the magic you create into *their* lives!"

From that day on, my passion for writing grew, and I began to write whole stories with complex characters but always with a happy ending, while preparing for university. Unfortunately, my mother died that summer after a short illness, during which I did my best to take care of her. After her death, I wanted to stay on the farm and help out, but my father would not let me. "Go be great! I'll be fine, honey," he assured me.

The next fall I went to university on another scholarship and took a job in the library. Between work and university, I had the good fortune to meet a publisher who was interested in my stories. "That's not luck, honey! The man saw a good story!" was my father's response to the news. And it so happened my first published book became a huge success, bringing me fame and a lot of money to pay off my loans and eventually renovate the stone house for my father to retire like a king. Because that's what he was to me. A kind-hearted king who was devoted to his family and was always brave, righteous and understanding. A few years later, my father died while working in the fields, not wanting to give up his work on the farm despite my many pleas.

More than thirty years have passed, and I still remember my parents' hard work on the farm to provide me with all the necessities of life, and their bright smile and kind eyes as they watched me grow up. And when I think of those days, I am convinced that they were truly happy in their humble lives. For they had always known that true wealth lies not in bricks and mortar, fast cars and luxury clothing, but in the richness of the soul. And what paved my way in life was never the expensive fountain pen and brown leather notebook that my parents gave me perhaps to make me feel worthy of the most extravagant gifts, but the gifted parents that life gave me.

About the author
Athena Constantinou is an environmental scientist from Greece with a passion for nature, travel and a love for all animals big and small! She has always considered herself a writer, but only in recent years has she started putting her words on paper in the hope that her stories will entertain or inspire others. She won second place in the 2018 Saugus.net Halloween Ghost Story Contest with her story *A Message from Beyond*:
www.saugus.net/Contests/Halloween/2018/Results/Adult/Second/

She loves to write, especially fiction, but also on websites, blogs, and to government officials to promote solutions to real-world challenges, because she firmly believes that words have the power not only to entertain, but to persuade and make the world a little better.

The Sealed Heart

Hidayat Adams

The vending machine came alive reluctantly, spitting out the coffee in spurts and drizzles, as if in vehement protest of having been activated. Hoult only stared at the cup slowly filling to the brim; he had been subjected to the whims of this particular machine too many times in the past to lose any peace over it.

"Finally," he sighed in relief when the coffee was ready. He took an immediate sip of the scalding brew; he preferred it that way. He picked up his worn gym bag from the floor; slowly, while taking intermittent sips, Hoult strolled to his office. At four in the morning, the hospital was just starting to wake up. Orderlies were pushing laundry baskets around, nurses harried the sleepy patients, those who were not incapacitated in bed, to get up and go shower or wash. Other nurses started going to those stuck in their beds to take their blood pressure and temperature. Hoult knew the routine like a veteran.

Upon reaching his small office, Hoult placed his bag which carried a change of clothes in his locker. Switching on the fluorescent light, Hoult sank into the chair at his desk. He instantly spied the white envelope waiting for him on top of the desk.

To Doctor Hoult Mesias: Urgent!

Hoult wasn't affected by the sense of urgency having been exposed to emergencies of one kind or another over these past four years serving as surgeon at Urion Hospital.

"When exactly did I become this jaded?" he pondered. He knew the answer to his own question, of course. He refused to revisit the time when he had lost his passion for his field. Despite his resolve not to revisit the past, his mind had other ideas. Against his own better judgment, he was dragged back to last year, his third year at Urion Hospital, to the time when he had turned into a cynic.

"The Board will definitely appoint you as the new Chief of Surgery. Mark my words," Lyle said to Hoult as both doctors were waiting outside the Conference Room. The hospital's Board of Directors was inside, discussing the choice for Chief of Surgery.

"You stand just as much of a chance as I, Lyle," Hoult said. "After all, both of us started at the same time and—"

"That's true," Lyle said, "but you have a 100% success record, Hoult. One hundred per cent! That alone is a guarantee that you'll be the Chief."

He was an enthusiastic person, a true optimist in every sense of the word. Hoult counted him as a friend, not just as a colleague.

"I guess we are about to find out how right – or wrong – you are, my friend," Hoult said as the door to the Conference Room opened. The secretary to the Board of Directors signaled to both of them that it was time to enter.

It was a bitterly furious Hoult who stormed out of the room a mere seven minutes later. Heat suffused his face; he was only containing his wrath with a Herculean effort. Hoult had gone only ten steps when Lyle caught up to him, having run after Hoult as he had left.

"Hoult! Listen, please," Lyle pleaded, pulling Hoult back by an arm. Hoult violently pulled his arm out of Lyle's grasp, but turned to face the man.

"I had no idea they would select me, I swear!" His voice was filled with passionate sincerity. "I was so certain you would be the one they would choose. I'm totally shocked by this, too!"

"Really? You're shocked, are you?" Hoult retorted, his tone dripping with sarcasm. "I should've known they would make you Chief of Surgery. After all, Daddy Dearest sits on the Board, doesn't he?"

"That's unfair, and you know it. The selection is decided by all the Board members, not just by one."

"Yes, you carry on believing that, why don't you? Nepotism always wins out anyway, doesn't it?" Hoult could feel himself losing his grip on his rage. What Lyle said next was a splash of ice cold water that cooled his fury instantly. It also left him empty and cynical.

"This is *exactly* why you lost out on the position, Hoult. In spite of being a gifted surgeon, probably the best this hospital has, and in spite of your success rate, you lack people skills. And your temper is another mark against you. Blame me, my father, the Board or nepotism all you want, but if you're truly honest with yourself, you'd admit that you're the only one to blame for losing out on the promotion. I still admire you for your skills, but I can't see us remaining friends after this," Lyle said before walking off back to the Conference Room, his shoulders slumped and his gait that of a deeply disappointed man.

Hoult felt his knees go weak; he hastily sat down on one of the benches located along the wall. He stayed seated for quite some time, absorbing what Lyle had said, and facing some hard truths about himself. Then he had shut down his emotions, sealing them in a steel vault, with no code or key to ever open it again.

Coming back to himself with a sigh, Hoult looked again at the sealed envelope on his desk.

This is probably as urgent as forgetting the lock code to my phone. Still, the letter intrigued him, especially since the envelope was not a hospital-issued one. Putting aside his now empty cup, Hoult reached for the missive. A knock at his door distracted him, preventing him from opening the envelope.

149

"Morning, Doctor Hoult," said Nurse Chantal. She was always the first to visit his office whenever he came on duty. He knew she probably had a stack of patient folders for him to work through. Suppressing a sigh or a roll of his eyes, Hoult smiled and gestured for Chantal to enter.

"We have the usual lot this morning, Doctor," she stated. "A number of urology patients, some for facial plastic surgery consultation, and three unusual cases."

"Unusual cases?" Hoult asked, his interest piqued.

"Yes, Doctor. We have three that seem to defy diagnosis," Nurse Chantal said, smiling as she did. She knew how much Doctor Hoult loved a challenge.

"Well then, obviously those are the ones I need to see first." Clearly that would not be surprising to Chantal.

"Obviously," she agreed as she handed the pile of patient folders to Hoult. "The three special cases are on top," she said before leaving Hoult's office to return to the Nurses' Station.

"Mrs. Joseph, I'm Doctor Mesias. I see from your file that you've been to see three separate doctors already, and none of them could discover what exactly is wrong with you. Is that correct?" Hoult asked the fifty-three-year old grey-haired lady looking at him with a gaze as sharp as a sparrow's. She reminded Hoult of the bird, too: small, delicate-looking, dressed in brown and black; black walking shoes, dark brown leggings under a light brown dress, all covered by a long beige coat.

"Yes, Doctor. I'm starting to feel as if I'm going crazy, especially when the doctors look at me as if I'm somebody seeking attention. I can assure you, Doctor, I'm no such thing."

"Well, the last doctor has referred you to us for a CT scan, which the other doctors should have done right from the start," Hoult said. "You complain of abdominal pain and some discomfort mostly at night, yes? Are you suffering from constipation perhaps?"

"No, Doctor. I am fairly regular and I make sure I get lots of fiber." Hoult asked the woman a few more standard questions before making his decision. He was confident he already knew what the problem was.

"Let me send you off for an X-ray first though. That might help us and we might not need the CT scan, which is more expensive anyway."

"I just want some peace, Doctor. Do whatever you think is best.

Hoult sent the woman off to have her X-ray done; the second case proved to be nothing more than a rotten, a *very* rotten, wisdom tooth. The third patient falling into the "unusual" category that morning was the true challenge of the day.

Before Hoult saw that patient, Mrs. Joseph's X-ray results were ready. Hoult called the old lady back into his consultation room to tell her what he had already surmised. He was puffed up with pride when he told her his diagnosis.

"Mrs. Joseph, your stomach is filled with an excess of flatus, intestinal gas. You really need to cut down on the fiber and foods such as cabbage and cauliflower. You told me you loved to have these for meals," Hoult informed a very grateful Mrs. Joseph. "We will give you a prescription to help release the gas build up. I suggest you stay at home when you take the pills, all right?"

"It's only gas? Now can you believe that?" Mrs. Joseph said, leaving the hospital a very satisfied patient. Hoult didn't tell her that what he would prescribe was just a placebo, as there really was no medication to relieve gas accumulation.

The last of the three unusual patients was a seventy-three-year old gentleman by the name of Thomas Barend.

He looked extremely spry for his age, having a full head of grey hair, wiry arms and a confident walk as he entered Hoult's consulting cubicle.

"Good morning, Mr. Barend. If you don't mind, could you explain to me what exactly is the problem?" Hoult had already read the notes, but he wanted to hear it from the patient himself. However, it wasn't to find out if the patient would supply him with more information; Hoult had already made up his mind that the patient was a hypochondriac.

He sat back with crossed arms and legs to listen to Mr. Barend talk himself into a corner. He was surprised though by what the man told him.

"You probably think I'm just another hypochondriac, don't you, Doctor?" Mr. Barend started, catching Hoult slightly off guard, "but I know my problem isn't just a 'figment of my imagination', as I've been told by the other doctors I've wasted my money on. I'm educated, not some boorish peasant who's looking for attention. The symptoms I experience are real."

"Please, Mr. Barend, tell me about your symptoms, sir," Hoult said quickly.

"I feel dizzy and weak for no apparent reason on some days, and when I went to see my GP he informed me that my blood sugar level was very low. Most of the time I'm healthy and fine, but on certain days, I feel totally drained of energy, and extremely weak."

"I see your thyroid has been tested and it's working fine. Do you have diabetes?" Hoult asked, knowing full well that Mr. Barend wasn't diabetic.

"No, I'm not diabetic."

"Are you taking any medications, Mr. Barend?"

"Yes, I do. I take Xanax occasionally for anxiety."

"Are you sure that's the only medication you use?"

"Well, aside from some vitamins and aspirin for the occasional headache, that's about it."

"Let me send you off for some blood tests and a CT scan. I would like you to return in two days' time, and bring your medication with you, please," Hoult instructed Mr. Barend.

"All right, that's not a problem," Mr. Barend said agreeably, leaving with a nurse to give some blood samples. Hoult also instructed the nurse to put Mr. Barend on an IV dextrose drip to improve his low blood sugar levels. When Mr. Barend went home, he left a troubled, mystified Hoult behind; Hoult could hardly wait for the results of the blood tests and CT scan.

The file on Mr. Barend showed that he had extremely low levels of sugar in his blood, but he wasn't diabetic or anemic. Hoult was irritated that he would have to wait two whole days before he could solve this mystery. Having seen all his patients, Hoult went on his ward rounds with a group of interns.

Hoult stopped at the bed of the last of his patients, Mrs. Michelle Theo. In spite of having sealed his emotions behind a solid, impenetrable, code-less vault, this sixty-six-year old woman had quickly become his favorite patient, surprising the aloof Hoult no end.

"Good morning, Mrs. Theo. Are we well today?" Hoult asked Michelle while he scanned her file.

"I don't know about you, but I'm doing quite well, thank you, Doctor Mesias," Michelle responded cheekily.

"Oh, we are in a playful mood today, aren't we?" Hoult said absently, not realizing he was once again using the plural form. Michelle would have none of it.

"Again, I don't know about you or your entourage, but *I* am definitely not in a playful mood. I'm far too old to be playful about anything. Just look where I find myself right now," Michelle said, gesturing at herself and her arm connected to an IV drip. She smiled brightly at a suddenly embarrassed Hoult.

"I'm sorry, Mrs. Theo," Hoult apologized, something truly uncharacteristic for him. "I'm a bit preoccupied today. Let me have a look at the drainage tube, please," Hoult said, lifting Michelle's hospital gown to have a look at the tube running from her excised left breast. She had had a mastectomy and was recovering quite well.

"Good news, Mrs. Theo. You can go home today. I will have one of these interns draw up your discharge papers right now," Hoult informed the still-smiling Michelle.

As Hoult was about to walk off, Michelle grabbed hold of his arm, halting him in his stride.

"Doctor Hoult, I wanted to thank you," Michelle said, her stark blue eyes staring straight into Hoult's eyes. She had no way of knowing that her gaze and the words she said next pierced Hoult's heart like an unpredictable lightning strike.

"From the first moment I met you and you examined me, I could feel your care and genuine concern for me. I knew I was in good hands, and this knowledge soothed my anxiety. Doctor, what you did for me… you have no idea how much that means to me." Michelle's eyes were swimming in tears. "I had felt that I had been condemned for some awful sin I must have committed, and had all but resigned myself to meet my Maker soon, but then you were sent by that very Maker as my surgeon. The tranquility that overcame me the very first time your hands examined me is indescribable. I can only say in all honesty that it felt like an angel had descended from heaven to enter your soul and guide you. You are more than my surgeon, Doctor Hoult. You are my angel of mercy sent by God," Michelle concluded, releasing Hoult's arm.

An absolute silence had descended upon the ward while Michelle was speaking softly to Hoult, allowing everybody to clearly hear her impassioned words of gratitude. Hoult stood as if transfixed, at a complete loss for a response. He was saved by Nurse Chantal.

"Mrs. Theo, I need to remove the dressing and your IV drip," she said, fully aware of Hoult's discomfort. Her appearance allowed Hoult to compose himself.

Smiling down at the radiant Michelle, Hoult said, "We are certainly the drama queen today, aren't we?" Then he surprised himself with a genuine laugh; his soul felt suddenly lightened, as if some burdensome baggage had finally been removed.

Squeezing Michelle's hand, he said, "Do you know what, Mrs. Theo? You've just gifted me something valuable I had lost a while back. I had not even been aware that I had lost such a precious commodity, yet you've managed to return it to me as a priceless gift. Thank you."

Back in his office at the end of the day, Hoult finally opened the sealed envelope. It contained a single sheet of crisp white paper. Hoult instantly recognized the handwriting as that of Lyle's. He felt a wave of guilt and shame cascade over him as he recalled his last interaction with Lyle. He closed his eyes for a few seconds in contemplation before opening them to read the letter.

Dear Hoult,

I know I'm probably the last person you ever expected to get a letter from, but here I am. I'll be brief and get straight to the point. I'm sorry I said those hurtful words to you a year ago. I make no excuses for what I said; I apologize for having been such a cad. You were my friend and I should have supported instead of chastised you. I miss your friendship, Hoult. I know we see each other every day we are at work, but it is a cold, professional relationship both of us maintain. I would like to change that, if you're able to forgive me. I know

155

it will probably be impossible for you to want to rebuild our tattered friendship, but I hope you'll be willing to give us, our friendship, another chance. I marked the envelope "Urgent" because this matter is that for me. Our lives are so short; as doctors we see first-hand how transient it is. I wouldn't want to go to my grave not ever having made the effort to mend fences with you, Hoult. I'll fully understand though if you choose to continue as a colleague, to maintain a professional relationship. I'm merely extending the hand of friendship in the fervent faith that you will clasp it.

Yours,

Lyle

Hoult was assailed by a gamut of emotions, leaving him breathless and adrift, like a ship caught out in a thick fog obscuring all directions. The foremost and most intense emotion was that of chagrin, followed by an overwhelming sense of guilt. Hoult rose abruptly and went to the bathroom to wash his face.

He stared at his reflection in the small mirror above the wash basin. He saw a man with arresting cerulean eyes, blonde hair brushed back, cut into a fade on the sides. Replacing his glasses, he noticed something else in his own gaze: a deep well of sorrow. His thin lips shaped a mouth made for laughter, but which was held in a permanent tight grip. His light complexion turned into a deep blush as Hoult faced his shame and guilt head-on.

Returning to his office, Hoult placed a call to Lyle. It was time to reconnect with a true friend.

Back home that evening, Hoult played the sound system softly, having inserted an Ed Sheeran CD into the Blu-ray player. He enjoyed Sheeran's soothing voice and beautiful lyrics, but he wanted the music only as background to his thoughts. And his mind was crowded with these. His wife, Glenda, was in his arms, as both lay comfortably on the couch in the lounge, looking out of the large window upon their garden. It was still light outside, the sky just beginning to turn a rosy hue.

"What have I done to be so blessed?" he asked her. "To receive two undeserved gifts on the same day."

"I've always been a firm believer in not questioning blessings," Glenda replied. "No matter the reason we receive them – what's important is that we do, and it means we did something right."

"I've been such a cynical, arrogant and stubborn fool this past year. I cringe when I think about my deplorable behavior. It was nothing short of an extended teenage tantrum, wasn't it?"

"Sweetheart," Glenda began, "most, if not all of us, go through phases in life. If we don't manage to emerge from these 'phases' a better human being, than we might as well forget about ever developing as a species. You've had your year-long sulk, and now it's time for us to move on to the next phase in our lives," Glenda declared, her tone conveying a hint of mystery. Hoult was quick to latch on to it, as he knew his wife so well.

"Next phase? Glen, what are you talking about?" Hoult asked her, sitting up straight so that he could look directly at Glenda.

Eyes twinkling and a wide grin plastered on her beautiful face, Glenda said, "I think this is most certainly your day for gifts. I have one for you, too," she said, her cheek dimpling with mischief.

Hoult got up from the sofa to go down on his knees in front of the still reclining Glenda. The palpitations in his heart betrayed the excitement he was incapable of containing, and he blurted out, "Honey! You're not saying what I think you're saying? Are you?"

"Yes, Hoult, my love. I am. We're going to have a baby."

Hoult's eyes instantly flooded with tears of joy.

"It certainly is true that when He gives, He does so abundantly," Hoult said before wrapping his arms around Glenda in a warm, loving embrace.

Epilogue

It turns out that poor Mr. Barend had not been taking Xanax, after all. From his blood results it was discovered that he had been taking Micronase, medicine used by diabetics to lower blood sugar! It was subsequently revealed that the pharmacy had mistakenly labeled the bottle of Micronase with a Xanax label. Mr. Barend went on to enjoy a healthy life.

About the author

Hidayat Adams is a self-published author of four short stories anthologies and one fantasy novel. He is also a poet who has had one of his poems published in a local poetry magazine called Stanzas. He is currently working on Part Two of his three-part fantasy series while working as an English Academic Support lecturer at the College of Cape Town. He is a confirmed bachelor living on his own; he describes himself as an "indoor plant". He bakes a mean lemon meringue tart and is famous for his fridge cheesecake.

The Veiled Maidens of Newgate Street

Fiona Clark

Madame Sylvestris, famous clairvoyant, put down her discovery of her special gifts and her success in later life, to a series of happy accidents. Born Nelly Jones, from Clerkenwell, she took on the antique shop on Newgate Street in Holborn after the death of her elderly parents. This was a convenient arrangement for her as her unreliable husband of seven years, who had seemed so charming at first, disappeared off back to France, with all of her silver cutlery and a younger woman (with suspiciously bright yellow hair) in tow.

"Nelly, my dear, I never trusted that man," Nelly's mother had confided, shaking her head sagely, she who had been simpering coyly at him so recently and sucking up his shallow compliments and sweet sherry-wine. Still, it was all one now that Nelly's mother had passed on and had a small white marble monument in Greyfriars cemetery, paid for by her funeral fund and inscribed with the words: "Beloved wife of the above."

Nelly soon found the business was running at a loss: too few customers came to call, and although she listened in vain for the jangle of the bell over the front-door, she spent her days polishing the bits of brass and dusting the aspidistra in the front room of the house, which served as the shop. Never one to give up easily, Madame Sylvestris (as she rapidly became known), cast about in her mind for a new plan of campaign. One morning, while sorting through the cluttered collection of curios, she discovered a crystal ball mounted on a mahogany stand. It instantly occurred to her that she might be, no, in fact, that she was (and, of course, always had been) a clairvoyant.

The craze for spiritualism was sweeping the country and Madame Sylvestris rapidly perceived that the antique shop was the perfect venue for conducting seances and private consultations. Customers, no, *clients,* could wend their way through the gloomy front room, cluttered with eerily ticking clocks (reminding us of our limited time on this earth), old portraits of frail young women with other-worldly facial expressions and a stuffed bear, looming in the shadows. The aspidistra would faintly brush against them as they made their way through to the candle-lit, private back-parlour, where the seances would take place.

Madame Sylvestris rapidly assembled the paraphernalia and specialist vocabulary of her chosen, no, *ordained,* profession. She had an abundance of very black hair, which she piled on her head impressively, leaving little tendrils to coil around her neck, to suggest a distracted air, the coiffure of a woman with her mind on higher things. She had an ample, matronly bosom (though the idea of children made her shudder), which inspired confidence. This asset she upholstered in dark purple satin, embellished with a long, fringed shawl and draped her hair-do with a mantilla of black lace. Through fine-tuning and delicate calibration, she arrived at a *Mittel European* persona, with an indefinable accent to match.

The back-parlour was a work of art. Madame Sylvestris contrived the perfect balance between mystery and intimacy: the low, round mahogany table, draped with dark green velvet and several polished spoon-backed chairs drawn closely round it; the crystal ball, placed neatly in the centre; muslin curtains framing the space and fluttering in a gentle breeze from an open chink in a hidden window, the gaslights turned low, soon to be turned off, then scented candles lighted, exuding a subtle perfume of lilies, all suggestive of a hinterland between the living and the dead.

All that was lacking was a base of *clients*, and Madame

Sylvestris' busy mind fell to work on this. By a second lucky chance, the antique shop was situated near to The Viaduct Tavern, styled as a gin place, with giant gilded mirrors and blazing crystal chandeliers. There was a "snob screen" behind which the more privileged drinkers could imbibe their gin, without contact with the *hoi polloi*. It occurred to her that she could frequent the Tavern and glean information about the clientele, who could be induced to call in at her consultations, where she could amaze them with revelations about their lives and their deceased relatives.

On the more salubrious side of the Tavern, there were murals depicting uncorseted young women, in diaphanous Grecian robes, labelled: Fine Arts, Science, Agriculture and Commerce and carrying the insignia of their callings. Commerce had particularly luxurious red hair and a sheaf of corn and distinctly reminded Madame Sylvestris of Molly Baxter from The Bull and Bush, back home in Clerkenwell. The seed of an idea settled in the fertile ground of Madam Sylvestris' imagination, to germinate at a later date.

Madame Sylvestris liked to partake in an occasional drop of gin, but her drinking time was an investment. She observed the comings and goings of the clientele, She identified the lonely ones and those with a weakness for a little more of a tipple than was good for them. There was a less reputable upper room to the tavern, served by quiet-footed Lascars carrying the bowls and long pipes associated with an opium den. The upper level also emitted unambiguous bumps and girlish giggles. Men sidled though the stairway door, with shamefaced backwards glances. No medals for guessing what THAT means, Madame Sylvestris commented wryly to herself. But she closely observed the customers to the upper level, especially the "respectable" ones. There's always a secret side to respectability and that knowledge was useful to her.

Next, she chatted easily to the bar-staff, tipped them generously and gleaned tittle-tattle, details of the daily lives of some of the regulars, especially the "respectable" ones. Then she had notices printed and positioned strategically near the pub doors, advertising the services of "Madame Sylvestris, Clairvoyant to the Gentry".

It wasn't too long before Madame Sylvestris' business caught the eye of bereaved clients, mostly women at first, trying to contact their lost children from "behind the veil", easily susceptible, easily consolable. Madame Sylvestris gathered a little conclave of followers, Tuesday and Thursday afternoons, who welcomed a change from their more usual knitting clubs, church socials and spelling bees. They gained a certain status from being Madame Sylvestris' "special ladies", a sisterhood, an inner circle, who had complete confidence in their spiritual mentor. They felt a fondness for Madame Sylvestris' spirit guide, a little choir boy called Eustace, who spoke through the medium's lips, when in her trance, had as reedy a voice as Madame Sylvestris could manage, and a high success rate in contacting relatives on "the other side".

But then one or two lonely gentlemen began to trickle into the back parlour, slightly shame-faced, often tearful. Instinctively, Madame Sylvestris knew that this was a rich vein to be tapped, but that more special effects would be needed. Gentlemen were less easily led, requiring more actual evidence, than "Eustace" could readily supply. Gentlemen also had more disposable income.

Madame Sylvestris went for long walks in the surrounding area. She was not fond of taking exercise but needed to do her research. Soon, she discovered a laundry not too far away in which young girls laboured hard, processing heavy loads of filthy laundry. Respectable work (by a whisker – walking the streets was often the next dreadful step) but exhausting and soul-destroying. It was to some of these girls that Madame Sylvestris divulged her plan, at a little tea-party for the chosen few.

The nervous girls sat on the edge of the velveteen-covered armchairs, with their trim of freshly laundered antimacassars (over which the girls cast a professional eye). In fact it was the delivery of the laundry that had occasioned this little impromptu party, on their only afternoon off.

"My dears," began Madame Sylvestris, "as you may know, I am a famous clairvoyant. I conduct seances for a refined clientele. The trouble is, I am extremely sensitive. My profession drains me, and I cannot provide results at every single session. Therefore, to keep my clients happy a little compromise is sometimes required, and this is where you young ladies can be of use."

"How much per session?" demanded Aggie, bolder than most.

"Oh, you will be amply remunerated-"

"Does that mean paid?"

"Generously paid per session, my dear, plus your bed and board at my house. Then there will be tips. From gentlemen who are especially well satisfied."

"Right, I'm off," Aggie declared, roundly. "I know what that means. I wasn't born yesterday. Come on, Molly, you are coming too. Respectable girls, we are!"

"No, no, my dears! You misunderstand me. Your task will merely be to waft. Under muslin veils. To impersonate the spirits from beyond the grave. Fully clothed, but without your corsets."

"How come?" Aggie was gaining confidence, now the self-appointed spokesperson for the group.

"It is well known among the *cognoscenti* – those in the know, Agnes, before you interrupt me again – that both

163

classical beings and spirits have no need for corsets or indeed, undergarments of any kind. Our gentlemen will merely need to verify by sight whether you girls, emanations in your diaphanous robes and veils, are indeed spirits of the dead."

"They'll try to feel us up!" snorted Aggie, indignantly.

"There will be strict rules. Under no circumstances will gentlemen be allowed to lay their hands upon manifestations."

"Manifest – what?"

"Manifestations. Spirits appear out of the ether, which is what fills the upper regions between us and heaven, and they are made of ectoplasm, which emanates from me, when I summon them."

"But we are made of flesh and blood!" exclaimed Cherry, who was amply endowed with both.

"Of course," agreed Madame Sylvestris, "but as I said, my dear, I cannot always guarantee a result. That is where you young ladies will assist, by resembling ectoplasm."

"But, will there be real spirits?" persisted Cherry. "I'd give anything to see my mother again."

Madame Sylvestris took a deep breath. "Of course, my dear. You will not be disappointed."

"What do you think, girls? Sounds easier than the blooming laundry, by a long chalk," proposed Aggie.

There was a rapid conference, a few doubts expressed, but all agreed it beat scrubbing sheets. Oh, to have nice, soft hands again, not red-raw paws and stinging elbows!

The seven girls were hired and supervised by Madame Sylvestris. As luck would have it, both Molly and Sally had sweet singing voices, to represent the angel chorus. Cherry was a bit plump for the task, but it was agreed that spirits come in all shapes and sizes, and she did have lovely clouds of ethereal hair. Agnes was rather on the tall and angular side, so was advised to keep to the back and come in last. Violet and Daisy had special potential as identical twins, for appearing in distinct parts of the room in the twinkling of an eye. Ellen had the blondest hair and saddest face, having lost her little sister, Effie, the year before, so she was likely to be the star turn.

And so, it began. The Seven Veiled Maiden Spirits of Newgate Street became quietly famous, by word of mouth among frequenters of The Viaduct Tavern and their friends. Most of the "gentlemen" were frail and elderly, missing their spouses, missing the human touch. Madame Sylvestris' rules were observed to the letter and the girls learnt to be as elusive as possible. Business flourished in the low-lit, scented back parlour. Angelic singing and portentous messages were delivered literally from behind the veil. Madame provided the information from her listeners and their gossip at the gin-palace.

"Your wife says not to sell the parlour clock for under seventeen and six."

"Your mother says she loves her sweetings very much!"

"Don't forget to buy the roses for cousin Mildred's anniversary!"

"George says to tell you not to blame yourself for what happened to Auntie Edna; the parrot was entirely responsible."

"Ow! Ginger-whiskers didn't half try it on," moaned Agnes. "Until I gave him the elbow."

"Be careful you don't give the game away, my girl," warned Madame.

"Madame Sylvestris – when do we get to see a real ghost, like what you promised?" begged Cherry.

"All in good time, girls, all in good time!"

Madame Sylvestris was in for a surprise herself, on this score. Slipping into The Viaduct for sixpence of gin and a reconnoitre, after an especially busy day, she decided it was time for a viewing of the old prison cells beneath the pub. It had been agreed between herself and the landlord that she would help to create a reputation for The Viaduct as a "haunted tavern" in exchange for his recommendations of her services.

"Business was better in my old father's day," complained the landlord, as he turned the rusty key in the secret locked door, behind a red velvet curtain. "You had the best view of all the public hangings in the square outside Newgate prison, from every window in this tavern, before they took them inside, on account of the crowds getting over-excited. Anyway, good luck to you down there. You'd better take this candle."

She took herself down the narrow stairs, with the guttering candle, avoiding the dripping walls and stumbling hazards. Once in the deepest part of the tour, a draught from the drop-hole, opening to the street above, through which kindly passers-by dropped food for the hapless prisoners, extinguished the candle. Madame Sylvestris was plunged into pitch darkness – then just that chink of light from the hole. To her complete consternation, she looked down to see the pale face and hollow eyes of a tiny child, holding out her bony hands and clutching the folds of Madame's dress.

"Give me food, lest I die," pleaded the emaciated creature, in a dry, tremulous voice.

With a cry of horror, Madame shook herself free of the child's grasp and rushed up the stairs, taking two at a time.

"A tumbler of gin – and quick!" she gasped, collapsing white-faced at a table furthest from the stairway door. Recovering herself, she thought, "Well, my girl – so you're not as much of a fraud as you thought!"

The encounter with an actual spirit gave her an unexpected

new confidence in her special powers, once she had shaken off the shock. She had an added spring to her step, rewarded herself with a new ruby brooch and hinted strongly to the girls that something might happen on the topic of "real ghostly presences" before too long.

Friday evening was the slot the Innocent Old Gentleman often called in for a seance. Tall and gaunt, he looked sad and spoke little. The girls had given him this special title because of his gentleness and the fact he never tried to touch them. He seemed to take their status as ectoplasm completely at face value. He also tipped lavishly.

This Friday in early January, the fog curled round the lampposts, obliterated the house fronts, enveloped passers-by in impenetrable disguise. This was a night for mischief and for murders. The Innocent Old Gentleman, otherwise, Frederick Browning, retired solicitor, alighted from a Hansom cab just outside the shop in Newgate Street, with his muffler wound tightly around his throat and his trusty service revolver in his greatcoat pocket. One could never be too careful in these times.

"It's just him today, no other clients, but since he tips more than a whole room of some of them, we'll go ahead with the full panoply of the Seven Veiled Maidens, girls," said Madame Sylvestris.

"Well at least he keeps his hands to himself!" snorted Agnes.

"I think he's sweet," whispered Violet (or possibly Daisy).

"Positions, girls! No more talking."

Silence fell as the girls assumed their positions with professional composure, corsets off, nightdresses on, veils fully draped, preparing to waft at the proper time. Frederick

Browning assumed his customary position in the polished carver chair at the green velvet table. Gas lights were extinguished and the scented candles lit. Madame Sylvestris made her grand entrance, in a splendid plum-coloured gown, adorned with the new ruby brooch. Seated with dignity at the green velvet table, she closed her eyes, intoning some phrases of a deeply occult significance. The voices of the Angel chorus began to warble gently from behind the muslin curtains. Molly had a nose-cold, but this seemed to add a certain poignancy. Violet appeared suddenly in one corner, a green phosphorescent light held strategically under her chin, then disappeared while Daisy mirrored her actions in another. Before long, the high-pitched tones of Eustace, the spirit guide, issued from between the clairvoyant's open lips, "Melisandre sends greetings to her dearest father. So do Georgina, Samuel, Amelia, Florence, and little Tobias. They thank you for the toys you put in each of their stockings for Christmas. They know the presents were the same as last year and the year before that, but it means they know they are not forgotten. Your wife Charlotte begs you to remember that life is short, but death is long and soon you will all be together. They all say: wrap up warm and don't get cholera."

Frederick never asked questions. He just sat and listened to whatever the spirits chose to tell him. The room was warm and homely in its way and the ectoplasmic presences were good company, reminding him of his long-lost children.

Then it was time for the Seven Veiled Maidens to emerge. From the depths of the back-parlour, a bronze gong reverberated mysteriously (Cherry's additional task). Slowly, the Maidens wafted round the table, coming close to Frederick and drifting their hands across his shoulders, fully relaxed in the knowledge that there would be absolutely no "ascertaining by touch" to follow. Clouds of perfumed incense filled (and further obscured) the semi-darkness, whilst the angelic chorus continued to warble gently. At one point, Frederick uttered a sharp cry, as if struck by sudden grief. The Seven Maidens paused briefly, but remembering their training, soldiered on. As the twenty minutes approached their end, one by one the Veiled Maidens evaporated into the ether (the tiny kitchen behind the back-parlour, in which they could disrobe and emerge in their usual day-clothes, to await the departure of the clients.).

Meanwhile, Madame Sylvestris bade farewell to her spirit guide, turned up the gas-lights and collected her fee.

"A guinea well spent, as usual, Madame Sylvestris," Frederick murmured gratefully, his mind still on his deceased family, all taken by cholera a few years ago, except for his dear wife, who died soon afterwards, from a broken heart. "And here's a remuneration for each of the eight young ladies, – I mean, donations to the cause of Research into Psychic Phenomena, of course."

"Eight ectoplasmic Veiled Maidens?" queried Madame Sylvestris, uneasily. "I'm sure there were only seven... manifestations."

"Decidedly eight," Frederick insisted. "I was surprised by the arrival of the little one. Look, she bit my ankle, the mischievous monkey!"

He bent down and slightly raised a trouser leg, revealing the top of his polished boot and above that, the distinct impression of a neat row of small, human teeth in his skin.

"Well, I can only apologise," began Madame Sylvestris, her mind working rapidly. That rebel Aggie, she thought, but the teeth-marks were so small!

"Not at all, my dear lady," re-joined Frederick, with a

sad smile. "It reminds me of family life. My own little Tobias was just such a prankster. Children will be children."

He glanced at his pocket-watch. "And now, Madame Sylvestris, I must take my leave."

No sooner had they exchanged courtesies and the shop door shut with a decisive jangle, the gaslights turned to their lowest setting to save money, than the clairvoyant summoned her Maidens with a yell. They trooped in, looking most surprised.

"Now, what is all this monkey business?" demanded Madame Sylvestris, far from her usual composure. But just at that moment, the gas lights guttered, burned blue and extinguished themselves, as if a sudden wind blew through the back-parlour. Before they could scream or speak, a strange, unearthly golden glow blossomed in the middle of the room, mesmerising them into awe-struck silence.

The golden glow quivered and resolved itself into the shape of a five-year-old child, a girl with long, fair hair and the face of an angel. She smiled, to reveal a full set of sharp, pearly-white teeth.

Ellen stumbled forward from where the girls had clustered together, behind the table. Tears were coursing down her cheeks and her hands trembled as she held them out to the apparition: "Effie! Can it be you?"

"Of course, it's me!" came the shrill, less-than-angelic tones of the little spirit.

Ellen held her hands out to the radiance and Effie held her fingers up to touch her sister's. All Ellen could feel was an intense warmth at her fingertips and a rush of sorrow, loneliness, and love, which she knew were coursing from her aching, mourning heart to Effie's and from Effie's heart to her own.

There was a stillness in the room and a scent of strange spices, spikenard, and frankincense, perhaps. Everyone gazed at the image of the two sisters, standing in silent communication, until the glow began slowly to fade and all that remained was Effie's voice, calling: "Farewell, dear sister, until we meet again!"

Ellen collapsed in a sobbing heap. As Violet and Daisy rushed to comfort her, the others stood rooted to the spot and Madame Sylvester hurriedly turned up the gas. But Ellen was not the only one with tears running down her cheeks. Madame Sylvester turned away from the wordless girls, to conceal her brimming eyes and heaving breast. Compassion! It startled her. When was the last time she had felt her heart so full of fellow-feeling? She had certainly felt nothing but intense horror for the poor little waif in the old prison cells. She held out her arms to Ellen. "Come here, my dear."

Ellen ran to the warm embrace of the tearful clairvoyant, who gently patted her back.

"It's the real ghost you promised us!" exclaimed Cherry.

"Indeed," said Madame Sylvestris, proudly. "Tea, I think. Aggie, go and put the kettle on. Cherry, here is the key to the larder. I think you'll find a cake in a large tin. Come, girls, Effie lives on, behind the veil, and we have so much to celebrate."

As they sat at the table, quietly absorbing their tea and cake, each separate mind filled with both wonder at Effie's appearance and a muted grief for their own lost ones, they felt a deep sense of unity. "My dears," began Madame Sylvestris, "I feel sure that this is only the very beginning of our adventures together. No, in fact, I can see it clearly." She was, after all, destined to become a famous clairvoyant.

171

About the author

Fiona Clark is a published author who writes poetry, short stories, playscripts, and who is currently working on a novel. Her work focuses on themes of nature, history, the paranormal and unconventional or transgressive women. She is lucky enough to live in the beautiful and deeply historical county of Suffolk, UK, with its heritage of ghostly hauntings. She is an enthusiastic member of Suffolk Writers group, Poetry Aloud poetry cafe and of Suffolk Poetry Society, with whom she publishes poems and gives poetry readings. She is also a reader/assistant editor for SPS online magazine, *Ripples*.

The Violinist

Abdullah Iqbal

The violin had come from her mother who had it made by Esbern, a soon-to-be master violinist who was only a fledgling violin maker at the time. People had thought it strange that a mistress of the violin would go to a newcomer. But, she must have seen his skill, his potential for the violin embodied perfection, an exquisite masterpiece, and every part was sleek and strong.

She is grateful for her mother's choice as she stares down at the violin she cradles in her arms as if it were a baby. Its sleek varnished curves and fine silver steel strings reflect the sunlight streaming through the painted windows. It fills her with a quiet joy. Her mother has often told her to keep it within sight and well looked after. She says, "Aletta: Treat it as if it is a young child, cleaned daily."

The first thoughts in her mind and the last thoughts to leave are of the violin. It leans against the side of the bed, within easy reach. Sometimes, she wakes during the night to find that she has grasped the violin in her sleep. Strumming a string produces clear notes of a type that passes into everything that hears them and nestles in its own special place inside them. The measure of a violin is the sound it produces. The sound of Aletta's violin is dappled sunlight, lapping waves, cheerful laughter. But it can also produce grief and sorrow. When she plays *The Sea's Lament* at festivals or inns, tears flow from the eyes of the listeners.

They say it makes criminals cry, heals addled brains and mends broken hearts. She is not greedy with her music, producing it whenever she can. Walking down through the streets she plays. Weather permitting. If it rains or snows, she shelters the violin inside the confines of her cloak to ensure it is protected. Barons, lords, knights and merchants are eager to have her at their balls and banquets but she prefers the inns. The innkeepers are happy to have her for they know that once she plays, the inn will be full and she feels like she can have true conversations with the common folk that come to the inns.

She plays with a fervour, her bow feels like the strings. The music twirls and scintillates, the dancing listeners who move faster and faster. Afterwards, someone always comments that it was a night to remember.

Aletta loves it most of all when she comes across a single farmstead as she moves between towns because strangers welcome her as family. "Treating a traveller well brings a bright future" is what they say. For a night she is one with them, sharing their company and a good meal. She pays in tales of the place she has been and music carries her on to the next village or town. Happily, she plays for strangers that she meets along the road, or just for her own enjoyment. Her memories of playing children's rhymes and music from stories and the joyful responses, help her to carry on going to the next town or farmstead.

On the road, where bandits roam, she is safe for they have no need of a violin and she never carries money for all money is sent back home. The music she makes is better than any weapon. It disarms her opponents in a way that a dagger or sword cannot and they leave her at peace. It also helps that it is blasphemy to attack travelling musicians, doctors and priests. Even bandits follow religious law even if they don't follow the civil laws. She returns home to Genice every few months. A few days with her parents where she helps to tend the garden but only for a few days as she is always eager to play the violin again before a dancing crowd. When she first picked up the violin her mother had been delighted. She had set a regime of training. Hours of practice every day, strengthening her fingers, increasing her speed and learning to read the simple yet complex language of music.

As a child, Aletta had been eager to learn playing smaller violins crafted by Esbern, those were the only violins her mother let her use. "You should know after strumming a string whether the violin is right for you. It should open a part of you, fill you with peace at its sound and a yearning for it when it fades away."

She has never told her mother, but all violins make her feel that way; it is the music that is played that carries her emotions, not the violin. If played by the right hands she is carried to tranquil seas or stormy mountains. Her mother has only let her use Esbern's masterpiece after many years. *Ah, the first day...*

"Heh, you with the violin, care for a ride if you play some music." These words break Aletta's peaceful dreaming.

He calls out to her from atop his thick brown horse, holding the reins. His face tanned to varnished mahogany, clearly from time in the sun. He stops beside her, his cart laden with goods. "I'm on the way to Holdcroft," he continues. His voice is clear and carries well. *Like a bassoon.*

"Sure." *Everyone enjoyed the music.* She hoists herself up into the back of the cart and settles down beside bags of grain and a smooth wooden chest. Once the cart starts moving along he talks, about his job as a trader in all sorts: grains, fruit, candles, rope.

"You name it and I've traded it," he says, turning round to flash a smile before he turns back to the road.

He talks about his sister, Mathilda, and their seashore

cottage. She opens her case and takes out her violin, *hmming* agreement at the right points. She tucks the violin in between her neck and left shoulder. The bow positioned on the string, eager to play. She begins with a light tune, *It's a Bright Morning*. She doesn't notice at first he has stopped talking. She moves to *A Sea Voyage* and then *A Bright Flower*. The sounds flow out, calm and collected as they fill their minds with images of glistening blue seas, wide meadows and white-tipped mountain peaks. Sometimes their journeys seem linked, sometimes separate but they are both lost. No, not lost, but willingly caught in the weaving of the tapestry – the sights and sounds of the music.

The sun is settling below the horizon. The change in lighting breaks them from their trance-like state. Aletta loosens the bow and tests the strings to ensure they have enough wax. "That was beautiful," says the driver, his voice raspy.

After taking a drink from his waterskin he continues. "I don't listen to much music but that was something special, even I could tell. You have true talent."

Aletta, used to the praise, thanks him, but he must have sensed something in her mood. "I know it's not much but would you be open to eating my food. It's just raisin bread and some cheese. If we were at home, I'd treat you to Mathilda's great pies. Would that be something? Maybe I could owe you a meal. If you ever come by Heatherdale?"

"That would be nice," she replies absently, as she massages her tense muscles and fingertips. They seem quite stiff. Loosening the tension. She doesn't want to get stone hands.

Her hands are always slightly stiff after playing. She's heard of musicians who lost the ability to move their hands at all. She couldn't imagine the pain, the inability to play. They stop by the side of the road. The driver starts a fire hands her some crusted bread infused with raisins and a few slices of cheese. She eats even though she wants to play the violin. She always wants to play the violin. Playing and playing... but she needs rest. The music masks the pain in her body but she knows once she sits down for a few minutes she will feel the ache return to her muscles. She never fells hungry. The music nourishes her body better than any food, it keeps her warm. It is magical.

She notices her hands are shaking. After she takes a few bites of the raisin bread, the sweet taste opens the hunger inside her. Keeping her manners, she eats slowly. Measured. In control.

"My name's Hai," says the driver. "I have been thinking of your name and it came to me; you're Aletta, right, the famous violinist. I never thought I would just meet you on the road. The One must be kind looking kindly on me."

She feels herself blush at his words but the fire must have hidden it as he carries on praising her music unaware of the effect his words. Something in his words touches her; she responds with a thank you. She feels lightheaded. *Why is she acting so strangely?*

They pass a few hours talking. Hai details more of his life as a trader. She is happy to listen, musicians have to, as they must listen as they play, open to the needs of those they are playing for. They seem to have been to many of the same places. She learns that The White Goat in the town of Crowfoot has the best ale and good walnut-stuffed bread. She learns of the cost of deerskins and fox fur. She interrupts his flow with a comment. "My favourite thing is freshly-baked bread with honey."

Hai's brown eyes seem to shine then, reflecting the last

177

vestiges from the dying embers. "I have some honey from my hives, it tastes amazing." He rummages in his bag and passes Aletta the jar and a slice of bread. She opens the jar; savouring its rich floral scent. *Lavender.* She places some in her mouth, feels the flavours explode *Rosemary and thyme mixed in with the lavender.* Hai smiles; probably at the dream-like expression she imagines to be on her face, as she tries to hand the jar back to him.

"No, keep it. It will go a little towards what I owe you for the music."

She protests but he places the cold lid in her hands. She feels the heat rise to her cheeks. *Must be the honey.* They continue talking well into the night, eventually falling asleep under the twinkling stars.

The next morning, Aletta rises to find Hai still asleep. She opens her case and caresses the strings gently as she cleans her violin and applies a smooth sheen of rosin. She always carries a few pieces with her for it can also be used to make a cream if heated and mixed with wax to put on wounds and burns. The thought oddly enough makes her smile. *She could be the healing violinist.* She'd used it on her herself plenty of times and it had always done the job. She helps to carry Hai's things and her violin as Hai makes sure everything is on the cart. He did say, "I'll do it" but she told him it was the least she could do.

Looking at the sun it is still early. Its rays shine through the scattering of clouds.

At least no rain. She stretches her arms and fingers, working through the exercises, making sure her fingers are supple and not locked. It happened once when she was new to it. She had been playing for hours and hours every day and suddenly her fingers had locked and refused to move; hovering over the strings. Her mother quickly noticed.

Aletta still remembers when her mother had opened her eyes and looked right at Aletta. Her brown eyes so calm. Without speaking she had come over and had taken the violin from Aletta and carefully placed it in the case. Clasping her hands she had simply said, "Don't worry, it means you need rest."

Upon her mother's touch, control had leapt back into her hands. She had hurried back towards the case eager to play, but her mother took the violin and started cleaning it, a clear sign that she would not be able to use it for the rest of the day.

"Do you want to eat now or once we get going?" It's Hai's voice. "I didn't know if you are hungry or not. I normally don't eat till later in the day." He holds a piece of bread in front of her.

She looks at him for a few moments before she replies. "It does not matter to me but thanks for asking." She flashes a quick smile and then climbs onto the cart, to hide the heat she feels rushing to her cheeks. Hai attaches the horse and they set off.

While they trundle along; well-travelled roads now smooth, weaving their way through meadows and fields, they exchange stories of their past journeys. Thoughts of home linger. As they enter a forest, the chirping of the birds and the gentle rustle of the wind brings them back as if from a trance. Hai then asks her, "Could you play your violin again?"

Happy to oblige, Aletta opens her case and rests the violin on her shoulder. She plays a tune that matches the eloquence of the birds. Their sounds seem to merge and grow into something new. The gentleness of the violin melts into the keenness of the birdsong. When it ends, they look ahead. The bright green of the trees, a lone dandelion by the side of the road. *Dandelion*? But it has a golden hue as if the music had enlivened its colours.

Hai doesn't say anything but listens as Aletta moves to the next tune and the next each blending with the sounds of the wind and the birds; the trees and flowers; to the sights and sounds of nature that surrounds them. Lost in the music, she doesn't notice the hoof beats pounding the road. All she knows is a moment later she is jolted from her seat. Her vision becomes a blur of colours and all she can hear is wood splintering. There is a sharp pain in her shoulder and then nothing but darkness.

Aletta doesn't know how long it's been when the a loud booming fills her ears. Slowly she opens her eyes and the colour returns. She finds herself surrounded by others, playing a variety of instruments from clarinets to bassoons. Someone is plucking a harp beside her. Only then does she realise that she too is playing, but her arms move of their own accord as if she is a puppet being controlled. She watches her surroundings and sees the elegantly dressed men in tunics and women in ball gowns as they dance to the music. Their footsteps are sure, swift and practised; moving in step with the music and their partner like a well-carved instrument. She recognises this place – it is Baron Ulhart's ballroom. But she has only played here in a band once. *She doesn't remember getting a message?*

Her fellow musicians seem to be staring at her; she feels their gaze and then she can see it their eyes – they hate her. Despise her. *Why? This was why she always hated playing in groups.*

The music seems to falter. The dancers seem to realise and their steps became less nimble and sure. She sighs and the images fade. She wakes up to Hai shaking her.

"Get up, get up." He half shouts at her and his blue eyes are streaked with worry.

"Are you alright?" He places his hand on her forehead. "Your temperature is okay." She feels his cool hand against her skin. She winces as the pain pulses alongside the coolness of his hands. "Sorry." He withdraws. Bringing her own hand to the pain, she feel a sticky warm substance. *Blood.*

"Where's my violin?"

A moment later she spots it.

Rushing over, ignoring a wave of dizziness, she collapses next to the already-broken violin. *No longer a violin just pieces of wood and string. The love and care of decades are gone.*

"I'll collect the pieces, you rest, Aletta," he says, but she doesn't comply. She crawls on her hands and knees desperately gathering up each piece. *What is Mother going to say? Can Esbern fix it or make a new one?* As they search through the wreckage of the overturned cart, Aletta stops periodically to hold her head. She slowly gathers the pieces of wood and string into a pile in front of her. Her head throbs badly as she tries to fit all the pieces together but how does she know what's missing? *If only she could do magic and reverse this. Make all the pieces come back together.* She holds the pieces and wished she could. It is beyond repair. She looks up. Hai is watching her silently.

"Did you say something, Hai?"

"No," he replies, and she returns once more to trying to piece together the broken violin while Hai moves through the wreckage, salvaging what he can of his wares, after checking his horse is at least okay. A roll of sapphire blue cloth, an iron chest, leather satchels. She had been so lost in her worries she had forgotten about Hai. *What exactly happened?* She waits until Hai has finished before asking.

"Some riders came rushing through; I think there were two but I can't remember their faces though I am sure I looked at them at the moment. They were wearing bright blue sashes and riding black horses." He hits a nearby tree with his fist. "I'd chase after them if only I had a horse."

"We could go and find him," she says.

"You are in no condition to be moving about. Conserve your energy." He is already moving away. "I will go and see if I can find anything."

She moves to get up but clutches her head and sits back down. She looks back at the ruin which is her violin and holds her head in agony. It no longer *exists*. *What will she do now?*

She watches her tears coating the violin strings; sparkling in the sunshine.

Some time later, Aletta dries her eyes with her sleeve and moves to the pile of things Hai has made. She finds his rucksack and takes out a wrapped loaf of bread and hard cheese. She takes a few bites and feels queasy. She places the food back in the wrapping, leans back and stares up at the sky; watches the clouds. *You don't have a care in the world. Would it be great to be like that just moving along... What can she do now? There is still Esbern. She needs to return home.* She can't hide from her mother. She plays the scenarios in her head. Her mother loved that violin. Had she ever thought of it breaking? Aletta hadn't ever – but her mother can help. She has enough money to pay for a new violin. She has enough stored at home to pay for a hundred more.

Fear grips her. *Would Esbern be able to make such a violin?* Her heart pounds and darkness surrounds her as she collapses into sleep.

Aletta's face is pressed against something warm and soft as she wakes. *A shirt?* As she straightens to look around she realises she was on the horse, arms around Hai. They are on the grasslands.

Violin? "Stop. Stop."

The horse stops.

Hai turns; looks at her. "What is it?"

"Where is my violin?"

Hai's face softens at her words as he gets off the horse and brings out the broken pieces from the saddlebag.

"So, it was not a dream?"

"Yesterday you mentioned that you are from Genice. I thought I would take you home." Her forehead is in excruciating pain and the last thing she remembers is Hai's strong hands steadying her.

Aletta wakes up under a woollen blanket, the light streams through the gap in the wall that looks out upon a familiar scene: tall oak trees and large meadows of wheat. The sound of the violin carrying its sorrowful tune enters through the open door – as if lamenting the passing of hers. She tries to get up but her muscles are too weak. She calls out but stops and listens to the music. *Will she ever be able to play as she did before?*

That violin had been hers; the thing that made her music great. Now she's just a normal violinist, without a violin. Worse than an untuned instrument at least that has potential. The violin is what made her great, what made her music famous. She sighs and stares at the ceiling. The music of the violin grows until it fills her. It sounds like her violin? A tear trickles along the edge of her cheek. No, it is not the same. Something seems to change, a sudden quickening and the music becomes fast but tempered, as if the player is on an adventure as they control the violin, bending the strings to their will. The music fades and is replaced by her sadness. She wants to play like that again.

A moment later Aletta's mother walks in; holding a mahogany violin. Aletta's eyes brighten. *Her violin?* Its strings gleam with vitality, but they lack the silver sheen and the shape is less streamlined. Her vision blurs momentarily as she wipes her eyes, but her mother knows her too well. She is standing holding the violin, ready to play. Her eyes say it all: *I know how you feel. I know what happened, but you have to get over this.* Her mother plays a slow tune, swaying with the music the instant she touches bow to string. She becomes one with the violin producing music but also something more. Unexplainable. *That is the thing Aletta has lost. She can only be one with that violin.*

No other will do.

"What have you lost but a violin?" her mother says. "You are the violinist. The violin is an instrument. A tool to be used by those skilled enough. The violinist produces the music. The violin can change but it is the desire and the will we put into the music that makes it great. I thought it was something you knew – I have not taught you properly."

That violin is the heart and soul of her music. How can she make something as great again?

"It's a good thing that violin broke. Now I see you still have much to learn. Listen, Aletta. It was only a violin." She pushes the mahogany violin into Aletta's hands. "Now play, play then you will understand."

Aletta strums the violin, feeling the hum of the music vibrate through her. *Maybe? Maybe?* She brings the bow close to the string but her hands shake, the bow is unsteady as it moves across the strings it produces only a scratching sound. She tries again and again but nothing. *Nothing.*

She places the violin down and bangs her fist on the bed, careful not to displace the violin. *Damn, damn. Her fear is getting the better of her.* Her mother walks over and takes the violin and bow. "Go for a walk," she says.

But all the walk does is tell her she has healed from her injuries. She has mulled over her thoughts but it does no good. She walks into the main room and finds Hai at the piano gently tapping the keys beside her mother. His large rough hands are at odds with the delicate music he produces. Her mother plays and Hai follows, copying each key exactly in time a half-second afterwards. Aletta stands and listens from the doorway. Her mother tells Hai once they're finished, "You have good speed and skill. You could easily learn to play the piano. A few years of hard work and you could make a good living."

He nods and sits at the piano while he ponders. *Hai playing the piano?* His bulky frame does not seem to go with a piano – but her mother is never wrong.

Her mother plays *The Tale of laila and Kiran*, a calming piece that her mother used to play. It tells a classic romantic story of a couple and how they overcame their differences of class and culture. A tune coming from the desert lands. Hai opens up his eyes and tries to follow along but the pace is too fast and after a while, he stops before he ruins the piece.

Aletta finds she can now relax. *She can still play.* She feels it. A surety. Hai has made her realise she can. Not only that she but she wants to. To connect to people on that level. Her music speaks for her; conveying words and feelings she can't show. Picking up the violin, resting on the side of the piano, she begins to play.

The shaking has gone. There is a momentary twitch of a finger. She plays, losing herself in the music – oblivious to Hai's shock at her presence or her mother's knowing smile. By the end, they have moved through numerous tunes. Hai plays after a while and his notes only add to the symphony.

A sharp pain pulses in Aletta's forehead. She clutches the violin as she leans on the piano. The music stops. She hears it calling but the pain blocks out everything. She opens her eyes; smiling. *So this is what it felt like to be injured?* The pain reminds her; she turns to Hai and asks, "What are we going to be doing about your carriage and goods?

He smiles. "I just need to get back home and I can start selling again. I'll be able to recoup the losses. Overall, I think I traded well for the opportunity to learn music and meet you."

She frowns and feels the heat rise in her cheeks. Hai touches her forehead. "You need a cold press." He looks at her mother who gestures towards the kitchen. After he's gone to look, her mother says, "Great job and a great man. You should be happy. He's a good companion."

Hai returns and presses the cold press onto Aletta's head. It dampens the pain. He smells like lavenders and mustard. Aletta moves towards the violin, but her mother takes her hand and leads her back to bed where sleep eagerly awaits.

When she wakes up, everything feels the same as yesterday morning. The same music flowing through her. No, faintly, she can hear the piano starting to meld with the violin. A cottage by the sea. Seashells and clear air. She shivers. Then falls back into slumber. This time she wakes to find a bowl of soup and bread by her bed. She eats then sleeps again. She moves in and out of sleep, her days a mix of dreams of a seaside cottage, playing the violin by the sandy shore and a man calling out to her in the distance. She turns but is never able to see the face.

After many days Aletta feels able to leave her bed and heads into the main room. An urge is inside her like a thirst after days in the hot sun. She plays but the music seems incomplete. It leaves her dry. She sits down and stares at the violin in her lap.

"Oh strings and wood and bow, why won't you give me what I want? To make others feel alive with music." She falls again into sadness. Hai walks in as she plays, and begins on the piano following the sheet music. As her music grows like a flower coming into full colour, the sounds of the violin crisp and clear and the piano deep and low combined, make something more. She looks into his eyes. Light blue orbs that fill everything.

About the author
Abdullah is an avid reader of fantasy, science fiction, philosophy and history. He believes that fiction can be both enjoyable and instructive. This is his first published piece but he has been writing for around five years though he does not get much time due to his work developing a cure for Alzheimer's Disease. He enjoys walking in nature and podcasts, and has his own called *Brain Explained*. He can be contacted through his LinkedIn, Twitter or Facebook account and would be happy to talk about writing or science.

www.facebook.com/abdulah.iqbal

www.linkedin.com/in/abdullah-iqbal

https://twitter.com/Abiqbal_1?t=VJ-IVwj3qAo_Po-LFcorMg&s=09

https://brainexplained725864474.wordpress.com/

Through a Glass Brightly

Steve Wade

A carpenter back in the day, before I took early retirement, I now spend a lot of time in the treehouse in the upper branches of the ancient oak. I first constructed it as playhouse for the kids when they were young. Long before their stepmother used her position to bend the law in her favour and gain custody of my children. Of course, I've overhauled the treehouse many times since then.

When I'm not doing a bit of hardscaping – replacing old planks with new, putting in further insulation, re-felting the roof – I use it as a place of refuge. Refuge from them. A place from where they cannot attempt to dissuade me from the truth and sway me with their lies.

They're everywhere. They masquerade as old men and old women who bid you *good morning* on early walks along the seafront. They take on the guise of cashiers in Spar and Tesco. They ride bikes or drive vans delivering post. As soon as they suspect you're onto them, they disappear and are replaced.

But some of them know I'm onto them. Easy for the unaccomplished to recognise those that shine brightly. Those of us who have been given the gift of knowing. Yet there are far too many who go about oblivious to this threat. Try to reason with these people and they accuse you of all sorts. The most damning that we're crackpots. So I've upped my efforts to enlighten the unenlightened masses. But how can you educate the ineducable? you might ask. Well, that's what Darwin did against the ideological resistance to his theories. And what Gandhi and Martin Luther King did when their teachings were systematically resisted.

Standing on the narrow decking outside the treehouse is my *Lincoln Memorial steps*. From here, I speak to those who gather outside my garden below to listen.

"We're being lied to by the state," I begin. I then go into my rehearsed speech about how most illnesses and diseases, including cancer, have cures. And how these cures are worth less than the mega bucks being made by the major pharma companies who peddle so-called cures in the form of drugs and vaccines.

Depending on the response, be it tepid applause, loud ululations, or the opposite, I follow a rule: I continue, or I reverse into the treehouse interior. This time there's one guy roaring up abuse at me. As if calling me names and using bad language negates reality.

From inside the eight-by-eight room, I wait for the heckler and the rest of the crowd to disperse. Back outside again, I continue my mission. I speak in a loud and clear voice without shouting. I advocate three things to the newly forming onlookers: "Resist. Resist. Resist. Resist what they tell you to believe. Resist what they tell you to do. Resist what they tell you not to do."

While I'm giving my speech, a woodpigeon lands on a nearby branch, I avoid looking directly at it. Holding it in my peripheral vision, I sweep my hand through the air before it. The operator of these drones manufactured to look like birds has no choice but to direct the drone to fly away like a real bird. I give them no time to allow the drone to hypnotise me through the bird-drone's eyes.

Perched up here also allows me to spy down on the Nicolescus's place. Lucinda and Masimo. From Russia and Italy, I think they hail. We've never spoken. But I suspect one of them might even be from Romania. They moved in next door last spring. My house is detached like their house. At ground level the gardens are separated by thick, two-

189

metre-high privet hedging growing on their side. Front and back. On my side grows a row of hawthorn trees. The hedging and trees combine to give total privacy.

I measure my day by the Nicolescus' movements. Well, at least I decide when to get up in the morning and when to retire from the treehouse in the evening. Lucinda and Masimo leave their house each evening as soon as darkness begins to fall. In the winter months, this is around 4.00pm to 4.30pm. While at the height of summertime, I often remain at my post till anytime between 9.30pm and 10.35pm. Likewise, the mornings. I stir to life at the sound of that big black car they drive, as it roars down the avenue and crunches to a halt outside their heavy wooden gate. Masimo drives the car as though they're being pursued. That, or they're in a hurry to meet or beat a deadline.

Those few neighbours I do talk to say the foreign couple work nights. They regard them as a private pair and respect their privacy by leaving them to themselves.

I, after much consideration and analysis, have figured the Nicolescuses out. As pale as a bloodless corpse, Lucinda's skin appears translucent when I glass them through my sixteen by fifty-two mms as they exit their house in the dying light. Relieved only by lips as red as seared flesh, her skin is further accentuated by the clothes she and Masimo wear, which are blacker than black. And Masimo with his thinning dark hair tied back in a ponytail, and his jutting cheekbones. It's obvious. They're vampires.

Fanciful is how I initially regarded my own vampiric conclusion the day it first occurred to me. Three slain flocks of hens in different farms outside the town, together with a missing fourteen-year-old girl in the next county convinced me otherwise. Gave me the courage of my convictions, as they say.

Stoats they said were responsible for the chicken coop

attacks. They would, wouldn't they? And the fourteen-year-old girl? Well, young girls go missing from time to time was the flippant explanation. Some elope with older men. Others disappear for always. The truth, they said. Tragic, but true.

"Not on my watch," I said to the so-called policeman I spoke to down the phone. I was calling anonymously to hint at my suspicions about the Nicolescus.

"Sir," he said. "Leave the policing to the police."

Thankfully, I refrained from warning him about young Hannah O'Neil. Through a fake account, I follow her on Facebook. The profile photo I use is of my seventeen-year-old son. He's a fine handsome lad, unlike his old man.

Five houses down from mine, on the other side of the road, is Hannah's house. I can tell when she's home. Like most teenagers, she hibernates half the day away when she's off school. The curtains in her bedroom stay closed. Lately she's been putting up Facebook posts reminding her "friends" about her impending birthday. That birthday is today. Hannah's fourteenth birthday. She's come of age, ripe and ready for that pair of bloodsuckers to awake salivating for her virgin blood.

From inside the treehouse, through the glass I've covered with one way window film, I train the binoculars on Hannah's house. After twelve noon and her curtains haven't changed since I last checked about ten minutes ago. They're still closed since she went back to bed around ten o'clock. Probably after getting up and checking her birthday presents. And sure, why not? It is her birthday, after all, and a Saturday. I'm sure she was pleased with the gifts I left in the porch: a mini rechargeable LED stun gun, a keychain pepper spray, along with a silver crucifix and a small vial of holy water, all wrapped up in pink wrapping paper with powder-blue butterflies and yellow daisies. The card in which I wished her *Happy Birthday*, I signed *The Watcher*.

Were it possible, I'd stay up in the treehouse for always. That way I could avoid them, their constant scheming and quest for global control. But sometimes I have to eat and drink. My shopping I've cut down to once, twice at the most, a week.

Later in the afternoon, I'm on my way to *Pincers and Claws* at the harbour. I need to stock up on fresh fish. None of your processed food for me, packaged, tinned, or dried, and all manufactured to slowly poison the consumer.

While away from my home and the safety of the treehouse, I alter my entire appearance the way others choose a different outfit – don't want to make it too easy for them. Today I've put on a small amount of eyeliner and sprayed on a fake tan. My hair I've shaved in a horseshoe style, what my dad, the bastard, used to call a *Friar Tuck*. A complete bald pate is too austere. More likely to attract unwanted attention than repel it.

I arrive at the fish shop. Outside the shopfront is the harbour beggar, Sandy. He flops about on his belly at the entrance, twists his thick neck to glance at me, then refocuses. The fishmonger comes out, ignores me, and speaks to Sandy.

"Hey, pal, why don't you go catch your own fish?" he chortles and tosses the grey seal a herring fillet. The seal catches the fillet and swallows it.

An old man walking his dog tells me that that's a good one, isn't it? And he repeats this dumbass-comment a few times. A passing motorist who has stopped to watch, applauds and laughs before moving on.

Bunch of clowns. Can't they see that the seal is a spy trained by the Russian military?

Inside the shop, the fishmonger squints at me while he sharpens a seven-inch deboning knife on a honing steel.

"There you are," he says. He scrapes the edge of the knife along the bar from the heel to the front. "So, who are we today?" he winks at another customer, his sneer twisting into buck-toothed concentration as he alternates each edge of the knife on the bar.

"A couple of gutted rainbow trout," I say, ignoring his taunt.

The fishmonger looks at me, still awaiting a response to his gibing. I stare him out of it. He gets my order. He knows that I know that he knows. Jealous, he is of my God-given talent.

"And give me a turbot fillet and four kaygees of Spanish sardines."

All business now, he weighs the sardines and puts them and the other fish in a blue plastic bag, tells me the cost and holds the bag out to me. "Cash or card?"

Do I look like I'm dumb enough to have a credit card? Just another way for them to get your details and have you under their control.

Unblinking and unmoving, I stare at him for a few seconds before taking my time to take out my wallet. And I deliberately slip out the notes and examine them carefully, like I'd never seen banknotes till that moment. I pass him a few notes.

"Keep the change," I say, when he puts the ten-cent coin on the countertop. "You can put it by as a down payment on some manners."

On the walk home, a steel-grey Lexus jeep pulls alongside me. I stoop to confirm the driver. Through the rolled down passenger window, I see Hannah's father's bespectacled and angry face in the driver's seat. He's shaking his head and his teeth are clenched. I straighten up and keep walking, my lips pursed, whistling Mozart's Requiem. This gets him. He drives on ahead of me and pulls his tank up onto the pavement. Out he gets, ready for action. Again.

He comes my way with his raised hand shaped like a pistol, his affected plummy accent collapsing in his rage.

"You're the one, aren't you? You're the one who sent her that stuff."

"And good evening to you, too." I say, twisting my wrist to glance at my watch. "Or good afternoon. It's not five o'clock yet."

"Listen, ye headbanger. You stay the fuck away from my daughter, right?"

"What are you on about now?" I make that face of astonishment. The one I've practiced in the mirror.

He rolls up his shirt sleeves, spittle gathering in the corners of his mouth. And he wipes the back of his hand across his chin.

"What are you going to do, hit me?" I lift my arms in a cruciform shape and jut out my chin like a cocky boxer.

In one of his clenched fists, he clutches a bunch of keys as a knuckleduster, one of them sticking through his fingers.

"Dozens of witnesses," I say. "Look around you." I sweep my hand at the passing cars. "You'll spend the rest of your life trying to pay me back."

"Keep away from her, ye fucking weirdo. I'm warning you." He glances at the passing traffic and storms back to his car.

Another motorist holds down his horn when Hannah's father's jeep trundles into the traffic. No indication. He brings his jeep to an immediate halt, challenging the horn-blowing driver to get out of his car and approach him. What a sad fellow.

He'll be sadder still if something happens to Hannah. But I'll do my best to make sure she's safe.

That very evening, I'm keeping lookout from my treehouse post in the last of the crumbling daylight. From my pocket I take out my pencil torch and shine it on my watch face. Almost 10.00pm and the bloodsucking fiends next door have yet to emerge. The front room of their house is illuminated by flickering candlelight. As it is every evening. Means they're still at home. Never have I seen their house lit by electric lighting. But what use would the undead have for electricity anyway?

Almost resigned to scrambling down the tree, I hear Hannah's distinctive voice, high and verging on hysteria. Her normal tone. I swing my binoculars about and train them on her. She's leaving her house, her pink phone attached to her ear. She's dressed in torn denims, a small white jacket and a tank top. Clothing she usually wears when meeting her friends to go to McDonalds. I've followed her before. But never at such a late hour. Surely her parents wouldn't give her permission to go out so late and, especially, to leave the house alone.

I shift the binoculars back to her house. The Lexus jeep sits beneath the wooden pergola, while their big black car is on the driveway. The mother's Rav4, however, is gone. Probably Hannah's mother and father both left together, giving Hannah the opportunity to follow her rebellious teenage urges. I must've missed it leaving the house when, overcome by lack of sleep, I collapsed for a bit in the old chaise longue I winched up into the treehouse last year. It also occurs to me that the Nicolescus may have likewise left without my seeing them.

Cursing myself aloud for my stupid slipup, I jerk the binoculars back at Hannah, as she disappears beneath the horse chestnut that grows outside the Nicolescu's house. I wait for her to emerge beneath the streetlight beyond the tree.

"Come on, Hannah. Come on," I say to myself, while the seconds tick by. Figuring she must have stopped to concentrate on her call, I wait some more. But after a lapse of too many minutes, a thrumming starts up in my head.

With shaking hands, I open the floor hatch and unfurl the rope ladder. Normally, I scramble down the branches, but this is an emergency. Hardly using my feet, I mostly use my arm strength and get to the ground. Out into the street I rush, but Hannah may as well have been the victim of alien abduction. Something I won't fully discount. Not yet. The street is straight and runs for a few hundred metres. And, as far as my eyes can see in the waning light, the pavement and road are empty of a young girl in a white jacket. I jump up and grab the top of the Nicolescu's gate and peer over.

"Hannah," I whisper. "Hannah, are you there?"

That's when I notice the dim candlelight in the front room peter out. I use my strength to pull myself fully atop the gate. I pause, using my hearing as much as my eyes. Silence. I then twist my body and lower myself until my legs are dangling. I drop to the ground with as soft a thud as my runners allow. Crouching, I work my way around a bed of lilies, brushing off the blooms, which release into the night a heavy and overpowering scent.

Metres now from the front window, I feel lightheaded and slightly nauseated. It is at times like this that I curse my unique gift.

I fight away the fear that conjures up images of a vampire's lair: bloodless victims, white as marble, their drained faces frozen in their last realisation of horror. Utter horror. Their eyes wide and their mouths drawn open in helpless and hapless terror. But then I see something that belongs not to my imagination but is as actual as the shifting scents that attack my nostrils – the stench of carrion mingling with but unmasked by the lilies and decades of decay. Two red orbs in the corner of the room, and two more. As though the owner of the second pair of orbs has been directed to my presence by its companion.

Turn away. Flee. Run. Speed through the night as if your continuance depends on escape from this deadly and unholy place. That's what every cell in my body commands me. I ignore the command. Instead, my fingertips touch the pencil torch in my pocket. I clutch it, free it, and bring it to life with a click, raise it and let its extended, sabre-like beam pierce the night and through the glass brightly, where it falls upon Lucinda and Masimo Nicolescu.

Unable to move, I stand mesmerised as I might were I to happen upon a pair of wolves on a kill, their muzzles red and caked with their victim's lifeblood. But the rhomboid eyes staring back at me are those of a middle-aged man and woman. And the white fangs dripping blood are theirs too. And laid out on the table is not a sacrificial lamb, but the lifeless body of Hannah O'Neill.

About the author

Steve Wade's short story collection *In Fields of Butterfly Flames* was published in October 2020 by Bridge House Publishing. His fiction has been published and anthologised in over seventy print publications. His short stories have been placed and shortlisted in numerous writing competitions, including the Francis McManus Awards and Hennessy New Irish Writing. Winner of the Short Story category in the Write By the Sea Writing Competition in 2019. First Prize Winner of the Dun Laoghaire/Rathdown Writing Competition 2020. Joint First Prize Winner in the John McGivering Kipling Writing Competition 2022.

www.stephenwade.ie

197

What's Left

Ellen Davis Sullivan

Two days later, the dog showed up. He looked dishevelled and smelled of some rot he'd gotten into. Sally didn't have experience with animals, but she knew a lot about cleaning things, so she picked him up and stuck him in the sink. In her grasp, he felt like a trembling handful of sticks covered in a doll's fur coat.

As he shied from her, she pressed down on his rump, which kept him from backing up onto the dish drainer. Once she ran warm water on him, he sat like Gwen did as an infant in her tiny plastic tub, chin tilted up like a princess resentful of being too small to refuse this indignity. Her daughter could always be cajoled into a smile when Sally sang old Beatles songs, especially the baby talk of *Ob-La-Di, Ob-La-Da* or *I Me Mine*. She'd smack her plump fingers on the water, her liquid drum set.

The dog remained rigid through the shampooing, but when Sally wrapped a tattered towel around him, his whole body loosened. She carried him to the sofa, where she sat with the towel-covered dog in her lap, imagining the queen just like this with one of her Corgis, not that this mutt with his crooked tooth and mashed ear would ever have his photo in *People* or *Star* or any of her other magazines. The weight of the dog's head against her ribcage was a pressure so pleasurable that she was dozing when the front door opened, and Gwen came in.

"You done with work already?" Sally asked.

Gwen had a habit of losing jobs, so her mother never knew if she was done working for the day or for good.

"It's 5:30." Gwen tossed her shoulder bag on the floor by the recliner. "What's with the pooch?"

"Frances went up to live in Moline day before yesterday."

"She left you her dog?"

"It's a long story."

"Just a sec." Gwen headed to the kitchen.

Sally dried the dog, and set him on the carpet. He settled down, his spine against her sneaker. She'd have liked to hang the towel out to dry, but Sparky lay there so peaceful, she set it over the arm of the sofa. It wasn't like the damp could damage old corduroy already worn smooth.

Gwen returned with a glass of iced tea, having made herself at home as usual. She slept on the sofa a couple nights ago after a fight with her boyfriend. Fights were common between Gwen and the men who captured her heart with their mix of rough charm and sly jokes.

"So what happened?" Gwen heeled the bottom of the recliner to make it rise, and put her feet up.

"Frances had been forgetful for a while, I guess, but no one thought much of it until she forgot her rent."

"Good ol' Doris: pay up or get out."

The property manager was a stickler. Sally'd had enough weeks when she was a little short, so her daughter knew how that went.

"Nita tried to help, but Frances was too far gone." Nita was Sally's closest friend, her only friend really, since Frances left. Nita worked for a lawyer in town and, after all her years in the office, she was like a paralegal.

"She couldn't take the dog?"

"The dog had run off to no one knows where. Frances's sister was in a rush to get back up to Moline. She had a place for Frances in a home. This guy just showed up today."

Gwen put her hand low to the floor and snapped her fingers, but the dog continued to snore softly, his whiskers like the bristles of a tiny broom.

199

"You keeping it?"

"I can't. Doris'd be here in a flash with one of her eviction notices."

"The old lady had it."

"She made a deal when she signed her lease."

"I could take care of him, if I moved in."

"I thought you went back to Red's."

"I can't be there. I'm clean for eighteen days. He tries, but…"

Sally straightened the pile of celebrity magazines on the end table, fighting an urge to open the latest *Us Weekly* and finish the story about Prince William, who might be going to marry that adorable Kate Middleton, though he was having trouble popping the question.

"Where'd you stay last night?"

"Out at the lake. I slept on Del's sofa."

"Nice of him to offer."

"He didn't exactly offer."

Sally knew how Gwen got when she felt her parents owed her something, which was pretty much always. She ought to make her daughter stand on her own, but it wasn't easy to do with a child who'd reached the age of thirty-six and still tottered and fell after every few steps. "How long you there for?"

"Del's sick of me already." Gwen took a pack of cigarettes from her bag. "I did get him laughing in the car yesterday."

"That's different." Sour's the word Sally would have used to describe her ex. He hadn't always been like that. It was how he'd dealt with his disappointments: getting laid off, marriages breaking up, the usual assortment of aches in the joints. In high school, Del had been a guy all the girls really wanted to date, not a football lunk, but a good talker, lean, sure of himself, a reckless dancer. And he'd wanted

Sally, a shock because she wasn't popular, though there was always a boy hanging around once she developed what her mother called her Barbie-doll boobs.

"He'll let me stay a little longer, but I have to start paying rent."

"I thought he was on disability."

"Still getting it set up."

"What's he living on?"

"Alimony from Wife #2."

"No." This came out louder than she meant it to, and Sparky started, eyes wide. Del, a kept man. That was the kind of thing that happened in Hollywood, not in Buckley, Missouri, though it would be like Del to still be getting the better of a female. She reached down and stroked the dog's head. He nuzzled the bent joints of her fingers with his damp snout.

"Course if you saw what's in his kitchen, you'd figure he's living on air and lake water."

"He doesn't feed you?"

"He doesn't even have coffee."

Hearing this, satisfaction spread through Sally. She wasn't about to let Gwen move in, but sharing food with her made Sally feel good, though a meal was about as far as she could extend herself. She was always surprised when folks confused her cooking with a more general kindness.

Gwen tapped a cigarette out of the pack.

Sally thrust her arm full-length, finger stabbing toward the door.

"Christ, you're impossible." Gwen pushed the recliner upright. At the apartment door, she lit up.

"Out," Sally said. Sparky popped up yipping.

"If you've got a leash, I'll take him with me."

"I don't." Sally hadn't considered how she'd get Sparky to do what he had to without risking him running off like

201

he did after he went out the window. Frances probably left his leash behind, but Sally hadn't expected to have him long enough to need it, so it would have been hauled to Goodwill with the rest of her things.

"Hang on." Gwen's sneakers squeaked down the hall to the front door.

In the kitchen, Sally pulled the pot of turkey chili from the fridge, and put it on the stove. The dog was already too much trouble. The Queen had footmen to do the work of taking out her Corgis and bathing and brushing them. Tomorrow she'd drive to the Humane Society and drop the dog off. As if he could read her thoughts, Sparky appeared in the doorway and looked up at her with his bulgy brown eyes. He ambled to the dish she'd set out for him, and polished off the last specks of food with swipes of his little pink tongue. He didn't mean to be a nuisance. Just trying to get along, like everybody else.

Gwen returned with a bungee cord in her fist. The scent of smoke wafted off her. She caught the ring on Sparky's collar in the J hook of the cord, and took a step, but the dog remained, butt down, his few pounds wedged against her. After a couple more tries of Gwen tugging and the dog sliding across the linoleum, she gave in and picked him up.

Sally pictured Sparky doing his business in the planted strip by the walkway. She pulled a plastic wad from her store of grocery bags. "Here," she said. "In case he goes."

"If he goes, I'm gonna kick it under a bush."

Sally stuck the bag between Gwen's palm and the dog's chest. "I don't want any neighbours complaining."

"You worry way too much what people will think." Gwen shoved the bag into the pocket of her denim jacket, wincing as if it hurt to bend her elbow.

"You OK?" Sally hoped her daughter wouldn't tell her something she didn't care to hear.

"I'll live." Gwen pivoted, Sparky's backside sticking out under her arm, tail waving like a mini banner in the breeze.

Saturday morning Sally met Nita at the Denny's for their weekly breakfast, or at least it used to be weekly. This was the first time since Nita's son died that Sally'd been able to persuade her friend to go out. Even though they'd talked on the phone every couple days these past few months, Sally felt near to giddy seeing her friend face to face. She was eager for the kind of talks they could only have in person, but after they ordered and the waitress poured coffee, Nita didn't speak.

Sally told her about the dog. "I feel sorry for him. He's a sweet thing, and I'm sure he misses Frances. It's really something the way he touches me."

"You've got a good heart." Nita stirred her coffee, the spoon going round and round.

Sally was about to explain that she meant the physical pleasure she got when the dog leaned against her, but praise was rare in her life, so she sat and let it sink in, thinking it'd be nice if it were true.

"I'm gonna hate taking him to the Humane Society, but there's no way Doris'll let me keep him." Sally blew on the coffee then took a sip.

"Tell her she has to. The dog's grandfathered because he lived in the complex his whole life."

"You lawyer types can always come up with something."

"I'm serious. Tell her it's the same as if Frances were still next door. Really, what difference does it make if the dog's across the hall or in your apartment?"

"He'd be cooped up all day while I'm at work." Sally hoped she'd be at the pharmacy all day, if things ever picked up enough for her to get full shifts. "I can't afford for him to pee on the carpet. If I had a house with a nice yard…" Sally leaned forward looking at Nita who set down her spoon.

"You don't think I'm going to take him?"

"Why not? You could keep him outside while you're at work."

"He'd be cold and wet."

"You could get a doghouse."

Sally didn't expect Nita to take Sparky. It was just an idea that popped into her head. That always happened when there was a problem. Now Nita's eyes were half-closed as if she had to hide what they might show. Her hair, always cut to a neat line around her face, splayed out in wisps. Neither of them spoke.

After the waitress delivered their food, Nita cut into her egg and began to eat.

"I've been wondering how long it was that Frances didn't really get what I was saying when we talked," Sally said. "Like when I showed her a picture in *People* of Alexa Ray Joel, who'd taken all those pills, I said how sad it is for a girl like that to try to end her life. She came back with, 'Don't I know?' – something you could say whether you understood or not. Even now, knowing she probably didn't, I miss her. She was good company, in her own way."

"I didn't realize you saw her that much."

"I'd go over with a covered dish on Sundays and a couple magazines I was done reading."

"Dinah wants me to come out to Seattle." Dinah was Nita's daughter, a successful business executive who did something with real estate way beyond selling houses.

"To live or to visit?"

"Visit first."

Sally's lungs clenched. She didn't know how she'd get

on without Nita, but she couldn't say anything that would make it seem like she believed she was more important than a person's own daughter. All she could see as she tried for a good breath, was herself coming in to the Denny's alone on a Saturday morning being shown a stool at the counter. "It's supposed to be nice out that way."

"I'm sure it is. I'm also not ready to make any changes... any more changes in my life."

Nita's son, Boone had been buried not three months ago after getting killed on a street corner in Afghanistan. Why he'd ever signed up for the military was a thing Sally couldn't understand. He was a quiet boy, not into guns or fighting, always tinkering with his tools out in the shed.

The shed. "If you took Sparky, you could let him sleep in the shed."

Nita raised her pale brows and gave Sally the look you gave a child when you'd counted to ten. She didn't say anything.

"I'm sure you could get a job real quick out West."

"Not as good as the one as I've got here without even a certificate."

Nita could have gone to college if she'd been so inclined. Last winter, she took an online class to help with her job. Sally envied her that. She couldn't concentrate on more than a magazine story these days. Sometimes, after standing for hours at the pharmacy, she was too beat even for that and flipped on TV to watch a home makeover program. Lying in bed, eyes barely open, she could convince herself she was in the crowd standing around the fixed-up house. The owners' shocked faces as they got their first glimpse of their new lives heartened her.

Nita looked out the window. Sally followed her gaze, but there was nothing to see except cars in the parking lot. It had never been like this between them, these silences.

205

"You OK?" she asked.

"Other than having lost my only son?" Nita's cheeks flared red.

Sally wriggled to set her back straight against the leather of the booth.

"They let him die on the pavement. Alone." Nita's tears came all at once with no sound. Snot ran from her nose. She pressed the paper napkin to her face and snuffled loudly.

Sally couldn't think what to say to the woman she relied on to buck her up when Gwen was too much, this woman sobbing like a child for all the world to see. It was more than a person could bear: Boone dead, Frances unravelled, Nita crushed. Sally stared at the syrup pooled on her plate.

She hadn't figured out what to say when Nita raised her eyes, the crumpled napkin pushed against her face.

"Sparky's such a comfort," Sally said. "The warmth of his little body—"

Nita's eyes flared. "You're the second person to tell me a dog could replace my son. When it was Frances, I could excuse her because she'd lost her damn mind."

"I'm sorry… I didn't mean…"

"You never do."

In all their years being friends, Nita hadn't said a cruel word to her before today. In the past Nita would make a joke if Sally didn't think before something dumb came out. Now Sally's skin burned like years ago when her mama'd take the hairbrush to her bare bottom for saying stupid things, like, "We'd have more money if you got a better job." Sally hadn't meant it mean. She'd believed her mother could do more than wash dishes in a cafeteria. Since then, she'd tried to hear how what she was about to say would sound to someone else, but mostly it just came out.

Nita stuffed the wadded napkin in her purse and took out her wallet. She put down money then stood to go. If

206

Nita didn't call and apologize before next Saturday, Sally would make sure they got back on good terms, whatever she had to say to make that happen. She couldn't lose her only friend over a dog she didn't even want.

In the VW, Sally set the dog in the passenger seat. He stutter-stepped toward her. She put out her hand to restrain him. Steering one-handed, she began to back out of the parking space. Sparky lunged for her lap. A horn honked. A white pickup filled her rear-view mirror. As she stamped on the brake, the driver gave her the finger with both hands pointing up through his sunroof. Sparky stumbled into her arm. The white truck passed out of view, leaving behind a memory of Boone in the beat-up white jeep he drove all over town. Her hand vibrated on the steering wheel.

"Bad dog," she said, but Sparky jumped into her lap, unbowed. He rested his chin in the crook of her elbow, staring out the side window, his sharp nails cutting into her jeans.

The road out of town started as two lanes bounded by pines on either side, low brush crawling through the spaces between the trunks. Past the woods, the fields were threshed and covered in dun-coloured hay. The only motion on the ground, the occasional skittering of a squirrel, would have roused the dog to bark if he could have seen it, but he'd settled into a curve on her lap, his chin on her belly.

Her grip on the wheel stayed taut, her nerves on edge from nearly running into that truck. She was also distracted by Boone, whose face she could now see clearly for the first time since he died. She ought to go home. Stand up to Doris. Say what Nita said about it being no different with Frances gone. Speak out for herself for once in a calm, reasonable way. All she wanted was to break a rule that had already been broken once. But she wasn't good at that kind of arguing. Her brain clutched like a fist. Words wouldn't come to her, not words that might convince a person as bull-headed as Doris.

She glanced at Sparky. His ribs rose and fell under his coat. She depressed the gas pedal. The dog didn't wake until she pulled into the parking lot at the Humane Society, and turned off the engine. She gathered him up. As she opened the car door, she heard, "Jesus Christ, look out" and saw that she'd pressed the door into the backside of a bearded guy leaning over a motorcycle. He must have pulled in during the moment it took her to pick up the dog and grab her purse.

"Are you blind?" he hollered, his eyes black, his cheeks flushed red.

Sparky started yipping. She said she was sorry.

The guy pulled a limp, furred creature out of the side bag of his bike. He stomped toward the steps, a large rabbit cradled in his arms.

Sally pulled the dog close and got back in the car. She leaned against the headrest as the dog's chest heaved against her. If she went in, that man could keep on letting her have it, not that she didn't deserve a scolding for her carelessness. She started the engine. What was she doing? She had to leave the dog. He needed a home. But she couldn't go in there now.

On the highway, driving into the sun's glare, she told herself she'd do better tomorrow, get herself more settled before she started out, sure of what she wanted to do.

At the lake, a large curve of blue water swerved out below the level of the access road. Cabins appeared between the pines, most no more than frame shacks, a place to park a rowboat, fishing nets, an outboard motor.

As she drove down the incline, the damp air carried a

scent of white cedar. Along the muddy bank, brackish water lapped the shore. Far out across the lake, a child sat on a wooden dock, legs swinging back and forth.

Down the gravel path, the jump of the VW's sprung shocks bounced the dog until he sat up as if to regain control of his slight frame. Eyes window-high, he strained to see out.

"Once we get there," she said. "You need to be on your best behaviour, just like if you were visiting Windsor Castle." The dog swivelled, and looked at her with his usual self-satisfied gaze.

Only a few houses had numbers tacked to tree bark. The rest appeared to be owned by folks who'd rather not be found. Number twelve's one was straight with the two swinging loose. Sally pulled in alongside a rusting pickup that once was black, now pitted and faded to a dull grey.

She expected to have a minute to collect herself, but Del sat on the screen porch staring at her. She lifted the dog out of the car, hooked the bungee cord and, keeping it taut, set him on the rock-strewn ground. She led Sparky over weeds and moist dirt to the foot of the stairs, three bare, wooden slats eaten away at the sides. He raised a leg and peed on the bottom step. So much for visiting Windsor Castle.

Del opened the porch door, the spring squealing as he pushed it wide. "Make yourself at home, why doncha?"

The dog popped up the stairs, chest out, as if he were being welcomed onto a red carpet.

"How are you, today?" Sally asked in the tone she used with the obviously ill who'd come to the pharmacy as a last stop before taking to bed.

"I'm about as well as could be expected for a man in my condition." Del looked like he did the last time she saw him at the Sav-Mor in the spring, a little more bent in his spine, his scowl lines deeper. Still, his eyes fixed on hers with his old intensity when he offered his half-smile.

"That's all a person can hope for," Sally said, aware as she passed him that this was as close as she'd stood to any man in a long time without a counter between them. A whiff of Jade East's spicy musk sparked a shiver. To be held at this moment would be a relief. Instead she followed the dog who tromped forward head down, sniffing madly.

Del let the door shut and moved to the metal rocker with a timid, uneven gait as if the pine floor hid nasty surprises between its slats. It took him a couple seconds to lower himself onto the rocker.

Having dropped in with no warning, Sally didn't feel entitled to make herself comfortable, so she leaned against the doorjamb until Del said, "Have a seat."

"Just for a minute." She settled in a chair, the woven plastic giving slightly under her. She gripped the cool metal arms. A murmur of voices carried off a boat on the water hidden from view beyond the point.

Sparky stretched his cord to the limit to get to Del. He nuzzled his leg. Del nudged him away, and the dog lay flat halfway between them.

"This is a nice spot with the view and all," Sally said. "You plan on fixing it up?"

"With what?"

"Gwen tells me you're getting alimony."

Del burst out in his old bell-clear hoot. "That's my girl."

Sally stared past him at the water. The kid stood up on the dock and flung out one arm, skipping a stone across the lake's rippled surface. "She shouldn't lie to her own mother."

"Gave me a laugh."

How did she ever find herself married to this man? Them being a couple seemed so distant that she couldn't recall what held them together for as long as they managed. She'd liked the feel of his skin on hers, though it was hard to picture this stooped man stretched out alongside her. It was what she missed most when they split: curling against him after making love, her spine to his ribs, her rump against his thigh, her cheek on the velvet soft skin of his inner arm.

"At least she's trying," Sally said.

"That's why I took her in."

"She does make a person feel needed."

"Not in a good way." Del smiled full on this time.

This was all that remained between them: a grown child who hung onto each of them to keep from falling into a life worse than any they could ever have imagined for her.

"Remember when you brought home that kitten for Gwen?" she asked. "You loved it more than she did."

"I did not."

"You called it 'princess'. You never called me princess."

"That bothers you after all this time?"

"I'm just thinking you might want some company." She jiggled the bungee cord. The J hook came loose from the collar ring. The dog was free, but still snoring.

"He's yours."

"I can't keep him. A neighbour moved. He got left."

Del rubbed his fingers across his chin. "I don't have money laying around to feed another mouth."

"He doesn't eat much." Sally felt a tear about to escape and put her fingers to her eye as if to get a speck out.

"That's why you came all this way?"

Of course it wasn't the only reason, but she wouldn't own up to how curious she'd been to see how he was living these days.

"Lemme fix that." Del nodded toward the bungee cord then he stood, grimaced and went into the house.

Sally put her head back. By the time he returned with pliers, she'd gotten Sparky onto her lap.

He pulled a chair close, set the collar ring inside the hook, and put the pliers' jaw around it.

"Not too much," Sally said. "I need to be able to get it off."
Del looked at her squint-eyed like he always did when she told him what to do. He carefully pressed the pliers until the J hook was nearly closed. She leaned toward him and tried to pull the collar ring out. Her wrist brushed Del's hand. The Jade East nearly overpowered her. She wanted to lay her head on his shoulder. Instead, she tugged hard, but the ring stayed inside. Del put his hand over hers and gave a sharp jerk. It came out. For a second, neither of them moved. Then he let go.

Sally reattached the link. "Thanks."

"Any time." Del smiled as he pushed up from his chair.

"I should go." She set Sparky on the floor and stood. The dog sat meekly at her feet. Of course, it was too late for that to matter now.

Had she hoped this visit would end differently? She had. She'd let herself imagine Del couldn't resist taking Sparky in his arms, and would offer to share the dog with her. The three of them would stare at each other with grins worthy of a place in *People*.

At the door, Del said, "It's good to see you're doing OK."

"Am I?" Sally pulled the dog toward the steps. He bounded down and headed to the car.

On the way home, she'd stop and splurge on a couple magazines and a proper leash for Sparky.

About the author

Ellen Davis Sullivan's stories have appeared in journals including *Cherry Tree*, *Moment Magazine* and *Stonecoast Review*. Her essay *The Perfect Height for Kissing* won the 2014 Columbia University Non-Fiction Prize and was published in Issue 53 of *Columbia: A Journal of Literature and Art*. Her latest flash fiction *Taking Mary Oliver's Advice* is online at Cotton Xenomorph.

Index of Authors

Like to Read More Work Like This?

Then sign up to our mailing list and download our free collection of short stories, *Magnetism*. Sign up now to receive this free e-book and also to find out about all of our new publications and offers.

Sign up here:
http://eepurl.com/gbpdVz

Please Leave a Review

Reviews are so important to writers. Please take the time to review this book. A couple of lines is fine.

Reviews help the book to become more visible to buyers. Retailers will promote books with multiple reviews.

This in turn helps us to sell more books… And then we can afford to publish more books like this one.

Leaving a review is very easy.

Go to https://amzn.to/3M3bC3f, scroll down the left-hand side of the Amazon page and click on the "Write a customer review" button.

Other Publications by Bridge House

Evergreen

edited by Debz Hobbs-Wyatt and Gill James

Life goes on. There is renewal. Nature endures.

This is a collection of challenging and thought-provoking
stories. All stories have an everlasting message and these
provide ones that will astound and delight you. We looked for:
story, good writing, interpretation of theme and
professionalism. All of the stories submitted had those
elements. Here we offer a variation to cater to our readers'
eclectic tastes. Sit back and surrender to the Bridge House
magic .

Evergreen is a themed multi-author collection from Bridge
House Publishing.

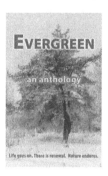

Order from Amazon:

Paperback: ISBN 978-1-914199-36-3
eBook: ISBN 978-1-914199-37-0

Resolutions

edited by Debz Hobbs-Wyatt and Gill James

Resolve is high. Determination rules OK. Human spirit excels.

This is a collection of challenging and thought-provoking stories. All stories need a resolution and these provide ones that will astound and delight you. We looked for story, good writing, interpretation of theme, and professionalism. All of the stories submitted had those elements. Here we offer a variety to cater to our readers' eclectic tastes. Sit back and surrender to the Bridge House magic.

Resolutions is a themed multi-author collection from Bridge House Publishing

"A delightful and amusing collection of stories from some very talented writers. More power to the short story." (*Amazon*)

Order from Amazon:

Paperback: ISBN 978-1-914199-10-3
eBook: ISBN 978-1-914199-11-0

Mulling It Over

edited by Debz Hobbs-Wyatt and Gill James

The Island of Mull, covered in mulls. To mull a drink. An important instrument for making a book. Plenty to mull over here. And plenty to make you think.

As ever, the interpretation has been varied: the Island of Mull, thinking about things, often quite deeply, the odd mulled drink and even something used in making a book - how appropriate again. You will find a variety of styles here and an intriguing mix of voices. There is humour and pathos, some hard-hitting tales and some feel-good accounts. All to be mulled over.

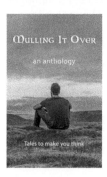

"The Island of Mull is a great concept - we all have had plenty to mull over in 2020. It's a great collection of stories. Very well done!" (*Amazon*)

Order from Amazon:

Paperback: ISBN 978-1-907335-93-8
eBook: ISBN 978-1-907335-94-5